INTERVIEWING IMMORTALITY

BILL CONRAD

interviewingimmortality.com

bill@interviewingimmortality.com

https://www.facebook.com/Interviewingimmortality/

https://www.goodreads.com/author/show/17088207.Bill_Conrad

https://www.amazon.com/Bill-Conrad/e/B074FFPZX9

Printed and bound in the United States of America

ISBN: 978-0-692-90908-9

TABLE OF CONTENTS

ONE 1

TWO 7

THREE..17

FOUR..35

FIVE...51

SIX...71

SEVEN...93

EIGHT 125

NINE.. 163

TEN 175

ELEVEN 201

EPILOGUE 213

ABOUT THE AUTHOR... 215

DEDICATION 219

ONE

Looking back on my life objectively, it was working out beyond my expectations. My divorce was finalized (again), and the third book of my popular *Grime* series had just been published. Best Buy gave me a fifty-cent-per-hour pay raise, my divorce attorney had gotten his last payment, and with luck, I would meet a seductive fan at my book signing.

Those were my upbeat thoughts as I steered my barely running, beat-up blue Toyota Corolla toward my future on that chilly Saturday morning. I had no idea what was about to happen or how a person like her could exist.

The bookstore was in a rundown '50s mall in Sandy, a small town outside my hometown of Portland, Oregon. The description my iPhone gave me for Island Books was "the best bookshop in Sandy." Unfortunately, it turned out to be the only bookstore in Sandy, and it needed a total fumigation. The shop was typical of the bookstores where I had been peddling books on weekends. This was by far the smallest bookstore I had been to, but admittedly, it felt cozy. The owner even had an old-fashioned mechanical cash register that made a "ding" sound when the keys were pressed.

The manager seemed pleasant enough, and he had a small, rickety table for signing books. Next to the table were three big piles of my books, and I was eager to sell each one. I asked if there was a decent place to eat, as I was committed to the all-day event. Small-time (or, as I like to think, up-and-coming) authors like me had to wait out the entire day, whereas prominent authors had a four-hour window and a line around the block. I ate breakfast at a greasy spoon and went back to the table. When the store opened at 10:00 a.m., there was a line of people. It was exciting to see so many fans interested in me and, of course, my fantastic work! I began preparing, by practicing my signature to make sure it was legible.

As soon as the door opened, all the people went straight to the used-book section. Saturday was "half off used books" day, and the manager was unloading a pile of new inventory. During the day, a few people came by my table, and some were actually fans of my books, or at least they knew the characters' names. Some asked me questions related to the book: How did I think up the plot? What was my inspiration? Was there ever going to be a fourth book? Why was it set in England? What was the deal with spell number eleven?

Some fans asked me totally unrelated questions: Whom did I vote for in the last election for president? What did I think about the old television show *Ren & Stimpy*? Did I live near

Tom Clancy? (Apparently, all authors live on the same block. Did they not know that he passed away?) What kind of music did I listen to when I wrote? And most of all, what did I think of their town?

I tried to answer their questions as best I could with enthusiasm, humility, and kindness. As I had done this before, I took great care to learn about their town beforehand. Book fans love it when you have a connection to them. The reality was that it was all an act, and I did not care about the people who read my books or the town of Sandy. My goal was to sell as many books as possible. To that end, I was going to tell them exactly what I thought they wanted to hear.

The day wore on, and it was getting close to closing time. I certainly had not met any fans who were remotely interesting. At all of my other book signings, there were rewards. I had met many fascinating people and had gotten many new book ideas. However, the low turnout and dismal sales made this an uneventful day with no bonuses. So I was happy when the store was about to close, and my day could end.

I was chatting with an older woman about the main character, Mitch Williams, in my first book, *Grime: The Big Hate*, when a woman walked up behind her. When the woman finished grilling me about why Mitch had not made better life choices, she left, seemingly unsatisfied.

The new woman immediately grabbed my attention. She had a completely wild look about her that flowed from head to toe, yet her appearance came across as wholly refined and sophisticated. She had jet-black, crinkly hair that flew freely in every direction, yet it was neat and presentable, like a controlled explosion. At first, I thought she wore a wig, but I looked closely, and it was her natural hair. Her face was well worn with crazy lines seemingly in the wrong places, but somehow this all worked together to form a perfect presentation.

She wore no makeup that I could see; her face had a wild, natural beauty quality. Unfortunately, some doctor had recently done less-than-perfect work on her nose and her ears. Her lips were thin but flush and formed a daunting smile.

The most striking thing about her was her eyes. They were soft brown, but they had a piercing quality. I will remember those intense, arrow-shooting eyes for the rest of my life.

Her clothing was utterly unorthodox, with a Sax-Fifth-Avenue meets 1800s-Europe look. She wore a dark blue, custom-tailored shirt with actual gold buttons that contained sparkling blue jewels. Her trim, conservative gray skirt was made of a material that looked like silk but had an unusual sheen, with a unique star pattern. There were no seams, or the seams were so fine that I could not see them. Her tan shoes had a stylish, comfortable look, and I could tell they were expensive.

Her hands were slightly bony, but well-kept, with fantastic, perfectly manicured nails. In addition, she had a remarkably trim, slightly muscular figure of approximately five-feet-four-inches with zero body fat.

Everything about her was a mishmash that would stand out in any crowd yet worked to perfection. The word "attractive" did not describe her, but her whole figure was over-the-top stunning. This woman was an enigma, and I did not know what to make of her.

I was trying to take in everything that was "her" when I realized some time had passed and I should say something. Her arms clasped tightly around my latest book, *Grime: At the End.* Even though my book had only been on sale for a month, her copy looked to be thirty years old. I stammered like a frightened pupil in front of the teacher. "I see you have a copy of my latest book. Would you like me to . . . ?"

The woman squinted and stared deeply into me. Really deep! The effect made me feel naked, afraid, and alone. I did not know what to do and could not move my fingers, cough, or even blink. A chill shot up my spine, my lungs struggled, and my muscles refused to move.

I have never been so terrified in my thirty-one years. The woman continued to stare while I could do nothing. Then she flashed an evil smile, and said in a wicked voice, "You will do."

I did not know how to respond or even what was happening. *What would I do? Was I in danger? Who was this woman? Was she crazy? What did she want with me? What should I do now?* I thought without having the answers to these fundamental questions. My instinct was to scream, but I could not utter a peep. The woman abruptly broke off her stare, turned, and walked away. She took each step with exquisite precision, almost like a gymnast during a precision routine.

While this encounter was brief, my shirt was sticking to my body from an uncontrollable cold sweat. Finally, I took a long, slow, deep breath. Eventually, the manager noticed my frozen expression of horror and walked over. I asked him if he had ever seen this woman in his store before, and he replied with a shrug, "No, but sometimes the crazy ones turn up at our book signings. It is part of the job. As an *author*, you should know that."

I staggered into the grubby bathroom that smelled like years of cigarette smoke and then locked the door. When I splashed water on my face, I looked into the mirror. A terrified person I did not fully recognize looked back at me. It took me several minutes to calm down and regain my composure. I tried to convince myself that this was the price of fame.

After the store closed, the manager took me to dinner, where he insisted I should pay. He was upset because he had only moved eight of my books, and the day was a bust. I tried to explain, "this is show business," but he observed that my book was "a steaming pile of paper pulp."

The manager confided in me that fiction writers were often a waste of his time, and the profitable book-signing events were home-improvement books. I felt indignant and was not sure how to respond. So I remained glued to my cheap vinyl seat and felt deflated.

The bookstore manager and I did not part on the best of terms, and I got the feeling I would not be invited back to the "best little bookshop in Sandy." But, I was relieved that the ordeal was over and I could go home. As I walked toward my car, I resolved not to set foot in this crazy town again.

TWO

It was midsummer, and even though it was 7:30 p.m., it was still bright out. I was full of greasy food and began walking toward my car in the bookstore parking lot. I noticed a tow truck parked awkwardly near my car. It was the type of tow truck that had a ramp, but this one was empty. Since the town of Sandy apparently closed at 5:00 p.m., the presence of the tow truck made little sense, but I shrugged it off.

I was getting my keys out and was about to unlock the door when I felt a piercing pain in my shoulder. I tried to yell out, but my body would not let me. My vocal cords and jaw were seemingly paralyzed.

Suddenly, a hand put tape across my mouth. I did not know what was going on, but I decided not to stand for this! I had taken karate in the fifth grade, and while I was not skilled, I knew how to defend myself. So I dropped my leather briefcase and planned out an attack.

I knew my attacker was behind me on my right, with a muscular arm around my neck. I did a quick right jab with my left arm, catching the person in the ribs, and used my right arm to plant an elbow in my attacker's face. Double-tap! Game over! However, all I struck was air, and this left me off balance. My attacker made a barely perceptible snort and swiftly put handcuffs on me.

It had taken less than fifteen seconds to put tape over my mouth and cuff me. I was furious and immediately decided I was down but not out! I knew I could kick really well, so I centered myself and got ready to meet my attacker. This time I was going to face my assailant. I dug my foot in the pavement to get leverage, then readied for a decisive, fast snap kick. This was my best move, and I would not fail! I took my time, mentally prepared my attack, and waited for the perfect opportunity to strike.

In the span of five seconds, I knew something was changing. The horizon moved, and I was looking at my feet instead of my car. Time had switched to slow motion, and I saw the sky beyond my feet. I can distinctly remember the orange-gray color of the fading sun as I went flying. Because my hands were bound, I could not steady myself and landed hard on the pavement.

My hands took most of the impact, and I let out an uncontrollable scream. However, the tape prevented any intelligible sound. Then, before I finished crashing to the pavement, my legs were bound with something that looked like a giant cable tie. Nobody in my fifth-grade karate tournaments had ever taken me down so fast, and I felt defeated.

I looked up, and it was her; the crazy lady from the book-store. Her outfit had changed; she was wearing a janitorial coverall. We stared at each other for what seemed like an eternity, and then she spoke, "It has been a long time since somebody has given me such a tussle. You should be proud of yourself. You . . . surprised me, and that is indeed rare."

I did not know how to respond, and the pain in my hands had sunk in. With one hand, she grabbed me by my arm and then threw me over her shoulder into a fireman's carry with no effort. *How could a medium-sized woman carry me like I was her clumsy purse?* While I contemplated this thought, the woman brought me over to the tow truck and threw me in. I tried to scream for help, but all that came out was a muffled "merrp" sound. The tape she used did not budge, despite my jaw muscles stretching my skin to the limit.

The woman had positioned me in the passenger seat, and clicked on a seat belt across my lap. She then hooked the cable tie to something under the seat, and my legs were secured. Then the woman put a wide nylon strap around my chest and closed the door. I was now at her complete mercy.

I looked over, and the woman walked over to where the fight (if that is what it could be called) took place, and she picked up my leather briefcase. Then she picked up the car keys that fell out of my pocket during the fight and walked toward my car. I watched as she started my car and drove it to the back of the tow truck. The reality was starting to sink in. *She planned my capture! Probably far in advance. I was in trouble, and my life was in danger. I would probably die a slow, painful death, and there was nothing I could do about it.* I cried, but the tape made it frustratingly difficult, which furthered my misery.

The woman put my car on the back of the tow truck and then jumped into the driver's seat. She turned to look at me, and I imagine my face was white with terror. There were streams of sweat and possibly tears. The woman stared at me with a playful twinkle in her eye. I recognized the message she sent: I have done this before, and you cannot stop me. Her look communicated all of this, and I wanted to say something angry or at least cuss her out, but I could not even speak a single word.

I finally realized she was talking to me, but I could not focus. I tried to concentrate. "Did you understand me?" I vaguely heard her say. She smacked me on the side of my head. I stared at her intensely, and she said again, in a commanding voice, "Do not poop in my truck."

What? What was she saying? I did not know. *What is this? What is going on? How can I make this stop? What does poop have to do with it?*

She stared at me and said calmly, "You are scared. This is true. You must relax. You must not get too scared, or you will poop."

I was horrified; only a killer would know about a captor being so scared that they would poop. Her calm voice sounded like a professional serial killer or hit man (*or was it "hit woman"?*), and I was going to be her next victim.

I tried to make eye contact, but she bent over to get something. I thought it must be a knife, and I mentally started preparing myself for death or torture. I was trying to think of what advantage I could muster to save myself when she raised a black object. She was bringing it toward me, and I was moving every muscle to prevent whatever was going to happen. She began unfolding a cloth, and I realized it was a hood. My world became blackness.

Then a sudden jolt as she shoved me forward. She grabbed my hands (which still hurt) and painfully manipulated my right thumb. I did not know what she was doing, but it occurred to me that she would cut my right thumb off! The thought of so much pain terrified me, and inside I was crying harder than ever. I prepared myself for the inevitable, and inside my head, I screamed for my mother to save me.

Suddenly, she let my thumb go and shoved me back into the passenger seat. I used my other fingers to confirm the bloody stump, but my right thumb was still there! The thumb check had caused my hands to hurt as the pain from the fall set in.

I still did not know what was going on, but I heard tapping. I realized she had used my thumb to get access to my iPhone. The tapping continued, and then there was the clunk of my iPhone being put into something. A moment later, I heard the sound of a seat belt being clicked. *Were we going to drive somewhere?* I thought while not knowing what would happen next.

"We are leaving now," she said in a pleasant voice. "Do you like music?"

I did not know how to respond, and as I could not speak, I shrugged. "Music is important in culture," the woman said.

I listened, and it sounded like a CD was being put into a player. *Who still uses CD players?* I wondered as the engine started, and we drove away. The music began softly and then grew louder. I had never listened to this kind of music before, but it had an orchestra with a distinct brass section. I let my guard down a little and realized that this tow truck had an amazing sound system. I then realized something else: she was humming along to the music. Her harmony was precisely in time and pitch. Then I realized her voice struck me as beautiful.

A bump in the road jarred me back to reality. What the heck was I thinking—her voice was beautiful?! That was a stupid thought! I had to figure this out. I *would* figure this out. I would live! At the very least, I would make my capture painful for her. I got my head back into the game. I refused to go quietly and needed a new plan. This is what I knew:

1) My abductor was a professional and had done this before.

2) My abductor knew martial arts.

3) My abductor was female with black hair, approximately five feet four inches tall.

4) She had a slight Russian accent.

5) Her looks disguised her age; she was between twenty-five and sixty-five.

6) The bookstore manager had seen her, which meant there were witnesses to her identity. This was my most powerful weapon.

Yes, that was it. Number six! The bookstore manager would call the police, describe her, and not stop until I was safe. *Wait, what? How would the manager know someone had kidnapped me? Why would he care?* The manager would read in the newspaper that I was missing and put my books in the bargain pile. He was the useless pile of paper pulp, not me.

What was I going to do? What did I do to bring this on? Then, like a lightning bolt, it suddenly struck me: My divorce. It was all so clear. My ex-wife had hired a hit person. This was typical of her: A hit woman, not a hit man. My abductor probably went around the country "helping" divorced women get their revenge. She would probably make a video of me apologizing to my ex-wife, saying it was all my fault that she cheated on me and spent all our money. I dreaded this hit woman thought, but it gave me strength. I had an edge in my mind: I knew the hit woman divorce explanation, and I would use what little I understood to gain my freedom.

We drove for three CD changes, and I knew each CD had a seventy-four minute maximum recording time. So with some major mental math, I came up with a radius of 203.5 . . . what? Hours? Miles? *What does 203.5 mean? Where am I?* I could not think straight; I was so upset and still crying inside, but there was little I could do. The woman remained silent, except for humming softly to the music.

I could tell that the woman's driving was precise and smooth. At some point, she drove the tow truck off the main road and changed to another CD. The music was soothing, but I tried to concentrate on my situation. The road was rough, and the CD skipped a few times. She was still humming along to the song, apparently without a care in the world. The humming was now driving me crazy. *Think of an edge; keep your spirits up!* I told myself this again and again.

Eventually, the truck stopped. I listened for other voices or any sound I could, but there was only silence. "We have stopped," the woman confirmed.

I heard the woman's seat belt click and a door open. I tried to concentrate on her voice to memorize it for later identification. A moment later, I heard footsteps go away and then return. Then, an unknown amount of time later, the woman said, "I am going to open your door."

The door opened, and the woman unhooked the strap across my chest. I immediately struggled against my restraints. There was a pause in her movements, and she told me, "Do you want another thrashing? Stop moving!"

I stopped and let the woman unbuckle me. She guided me out of the truck. The hood still covered my eyes, and I did not know where to put my feet, but I could tell I was on a dirt surface. The woman made a "hmm" sound and said, "Good, you did not poop."

I was still horrified, but I chuckled. The woman heard me, and it must have amused her because she let out a barely perceptible snort.

The woman guided me along, but the foot restraints limited my mobility. Soon we went up three steps and then through a door. My hands really hurt, but I still had my wits, and I was prepared (well, at least in my mind) for anything. I soon noticed a smell; it was wonderful, like a bakery. She led me through what I assumed were hallways, and then we came to a stop. So this was it: We were in a bakery, and I would be turned into pie and then eaten, like in the play *Sweeney Todd*.

I decided I would not be made into a pie! I formed a plan to make some sort of headbutt and only needed a target. She had me sit down on something soft, and I heard her footsteps as she left for a moment. She came back and said quietly, "I'm lighting the lamps. Prepare your eyes for light."

The woman took the hood off, and I found myself in a small bedroom with minimal accommodations. The room was lit by two small oil lamps, which did not make sense. The bed looked like it belonged in a mental hospital, with big, leather tie-down straps. She adopted a concerned look and stated firmly, "Lie back, and I will tuck you in."

I stared at the woman while looking for the perfect opportunity to punch her with all my might. Next, she took my right leg and attached it to the bed strap without undoing the cable tie. The woman then took my left leg, loosened the strap, and then attached it to my leg in such a way that it could not move. She then cut the cable tie with a small knife. After that, my legs began feeling better.

In a burst of speed, the woman was behind me. She grabbed my left hand in a pinch hold and then took my right hand. Somehow, the woman undid the handcuffs. I could not visualize how she was keeping me restrained while taking off the handcuffs. The woman guided my right hand to the strap and affixed it. She then guided my left hand, and I was totally secure.

The woman got up, stood beside me, and sounded amused as she said, "This is going to be painful. You must not scream."

I did not know what she meant until she ripped the tape off my mouth. *Wow, did that hurt!* I had somehow forgotten about the tape and was sure all of my lip skin had come off.

I turned to the woman and yelled, "Hey, that was mean!"

The woman smirked and said firmly, "Get a good night's rest. Tomorrow will be a big day for you."

The woman stood up to leave, and I called out, "Wait, what is going on? Is this like the book *Misery* by Stephen King?"

The woman's face turned into a question mark, and I filled in the blanks, "You know, the one where the book fan kidnaps the author and makes him write a different ending?"

The woman's head shake was barely perceptible as she said, "You give yourself much too much credit. Get some sleep."

With that, the woman left and locked the door. I had a million questions without answers. I took stock of the situation, and the only thing I knew for sure was that I was alive. I vowed to stay awake and develop a new plan, but I fell asleep in minutes.

THREE

I noticed something, but I did not know what. Then I realized I was being shaken. It was my left leg, and I could hear, "You snore. Time to get up."

When I opened my eyes, the woman was standing over me. She dressed in what I could only describe as a gray chef's outfit. The woman's hair had changed from crinkled jet black to straight soft brown. It was neatly tied back in a tight braid. There was a white substance on the woman's left sleeve. The lines in her face were gone, and her nose and ears looked much better. The woman's eyes were still soft brown, piercing, and shooting question-mark arrows at me. She still completely intimidated me.

The woman was holding a leather restraining cuff and tied my feet together so that I had limited leg movement. She also attached a small lock so I could not undo the leg restraints.

Next, the woman slid a restraining cuff around my waist and restrained my left hand with another lock. She then undid the bed restraints and said firmly, "You now have one hand free. You may use the restroom."

I stared at her without knowing what to say and got up. Then, because I gained a bit of composure, I asked sarcastically, "What, no good morning?"

The woman gave a quick, painful jab to my solar plexus. My karate teacher used to do that when I talked back to him. I doubled over in pain. She led me down the hall to a nice but small restroom. Inside, there was some natural light, but oil lamps provided most of the illumination. I then realized that my watch was missing. *How did she get my watch off?* I did not know what time it was. Once inside, I turned around. The woman was right there and said firmly, "Clean yourself up. Do not cause mischief."

I stared at her, and she closed the door. When I turned around, I saw a disposable razor, soap, and a toothbrush on the sink. Immediately, I thought, *I can use this razor to cut her and win my freedom.* But I looked in the mirror and saw my face for the first time. There was a big red mark where the tape had been. I had a bruise above my eye and did not recall being hit there. My body hurt everywhere.

I turned on the sink and listened to the water going down the drain. The magnitude of what was going on hit me all at once, and I stared at myself. Then, there was a bang on the door, and the woman yelled, "Do not waste water! I pay for that!"

That brought me out of my self-pity, and I began washing. After that, I used the toilet and did a quick shave. Then, I called out to the woman, "I would like to take a shower."

"Not now," she responded in an angry voice. "Later."

Well, at least I had tried. I thought as I washed my face and looked in the mirror at my shaven face. It looked rough, tired, and not very handsome. I brushed my hair with my hand as best I could.

I was as ready as I could be for whatever was ahead. I opened the door, and the woman was there, staring at me. Then, without breaking the stare, she asked, "Did you take the blade out of the razor?"

I pointed to the razor on the sink and shook my head. The woman made a slight grunting sound and led me down the hall. One thing had been puzzling me. There were no light fixtures or outlets in the walls. It occurred to me that this building must be far away from any town. It had a slightly musty odor but was otherwise spotless.

We came to a kitchen. It was amazing—a big, open area with lots of workspace, two stoves, a huge stainless-steel refrigerator, wire baskets, fresh vegetables, ten different rolling pins, thirty hanging pots, and huge shelves of dry food. The absolute precision of this room stunned me, and I remarked, "This is a really nice kitchen."

Without looking at me, the woman replied in an amused voice, "Thank you."

"I don't see any electricity. How does the refrigerator work?"

The woman stared at me with an annoyed expression but did not answer my question. We continued our walk and entered a medium-size room with a dining table. It held an elegant spread of food that included fresh bread, pastries, chicken dumplings, omelets, four kinds of juice, and a silver coffee pot.

The plates had the most amazing finish with an elaborate, inlaid gold-and-silver pattern. The silverware was made of silver, and the coffee spoons appeared to be solid gold with stones that looked like real emeralds embedded in the end. The fine, white, embroidered, custom-fit linen tablecloth did not have a single wrinkle or spot. I had never experienced such class and refinement.

I did not know what to do next and discretely looked around. The woman sat down and motioned with her hand to the chair across from her. I stared at her, and she motioned again. The woman then said, sounding slightly irritated, "You should not stare at me as you do. That kind of behavior is not polite. Please eat up. You have a big day ahead of you."

"Look," I replied. "I want to know what is going on, but I won't do anything until I get some answers!"

I was putting my foot down and trying to take control of the situation. The woman gave me a cross expression and said firmly, "Eat first, and then we will talk. You will need strength."

I stared back at her, looked down at the plate, and realized that there was not a single scratch. I could tell quality, and this brand-new plate must have cost over a hundred bucks. I decided to eat something to get my mind back into the game. I realized I could smash the plate in defiance, but I looked up at the woman, and she seemed to read my thoughts. She sent me a look that explained the pain I would endure if I tried something reckless.

With my one free hand, I took a thin roll and poured some juice and coffee. I noticed the woman was giving me an evil stare. I did not know what I had done wrong and asked, "Should I have said grace?"

The woman looked down at my plate, and I realized I had not placed my napkin in my lap. So I placed it on my legs, and her expression changed. It suddenly occurred to me that the food could be poison, so I waited for her to eat.

With extreme elegance, the woman poured a cup of tea and placed a currant scone and a small portion of omelet on her plate. While she did this, her eyes kept flashing in my direction, as if she was asking questions and then quickly ascertaining the answers. The woman used a fork and knife to pick up a small corner of the scone. Her eating technique was a symphony of refinement. The woman's hand movements were precise and flawless. I pondered this for a while, picked up my coffee cup, and took a small sip. I was shocked beyond belief. The coffee was over-the-top outstanding, and I had never tasted a beverage so fresh and rich. I looked over at the woman and saw another barely perceptible smile.

I decided to try some polite conversation and asked, "Did you make all this food yourself?"

The woman nodded between slow sips of her tea. Finally, I blurted out, "You're an excellent cook."

The woman tilted her head to the right and smiled slightly as if to say thank you. Then I tasted the bread; that must have been what I had smelled the night before. It crunched and then melted in my mouth. It was like I had been born and was eating solid food for the first time. The first juice I tried was raspberry. It was beyond outstanding and obviously fresh.

I looked over, and the woman was carefully eating portions of her scone. I tried my best to be civil and eat manageable portions, but it was difficult. Even the butter was crazy good;

I could eat a carload with no regrets. It was so creamy I could even take a bath in the butter.

The food taste was removing all sense of reality. However, I got my game back together and tried another attempt at casual conversation. In my most pleasant voice, I said, "I realized I don't know your name. I'm James Kimble, but my friends call me J.K."

Another barely perceptible nod, and I continued my one-sided conversation. "You have put a lot of effort into this meal. It's like eating in a private room at a five-star restaurant. I don't know when I have ever had such good food."

Another barely perceptible nod and I could tell that the woman was growing frustrated, but I did not know what mistake I had made. She looked at me between bites of what I assume was jam on toast points and then spoke, "You should thoroughly enjoy your food. Eat slowly and savor."

I slowed my eating down and ate small bites while chewing for a long time. This seemed to satisfy the woman, but my poor manners were clearly upsetting her.

When it appeared that our meal was over, the woman got up. I got up too, but I forgot to put my napkin on the table, and it fell to the floor. I reached down to get it, and in the blink of an eye, she was behind me. I perceived she had a knife in my back, and I blurted out, "Ahhh . . . napkin?"

The woman was unhappy but appeared to be satisfied with this explanation, so she moved away. Then I casually asked, "May I help with the dishes?"

For the first time, I saw a "normal person" smile appear on the woman's face. My mother had forced it into me to always offer to do the dishes when invited to dinner. Her smile lasted a mere moment, then she put her hand on my shoulder and spoke quietly, "That's twice you surprised me. I'll take care of the dishes. We have much to discuss."

At this point, I would not say I was comfortable, but I was no longer terrified. The woman said quietly, "Would you like to freshen up?"

I nodded, and she pointed to the bathroom. She did not follow, and for the first time, I noticed doors along the hallway. I was tempted to open them, but the voice in my head screamed not to. My voice rarely spoke, but when it did, I listened because it was usually correct. However, more than once, that voice got me into the principal's office. It also got me married, and that was not my best decision.

In the bathroom, the razor was no longer there. *How did she take it? Were we alone?* I thought and then realized she did not do all the cooking. It occurred to me that this entire situation must be a game or television reality show. I looked for cameras and microphones, but I did not see any. I knew they must be there—I was not looking hard enough.

After more searching for television show evidence, I gave up and splashed water on my face. After I relieved myself, I tried to regain some composure. I noticed that the soft blue towels were hand-embroidered with gold thread. They were the softest towels I have ever felt; they must have cost a week's salary each. *How does she afford all of this? Who puts these kinds of expensive towels in a guest bathroom?* I still had so many questions but no answers. However, I was making some headway and building a connection with the woman.

I left the bathroom and made my way to the kitchen. The dining room was now spotlessly clean. I stood there and wondered how a single person could clean up so quickly; then, I realized the "staff" must have done it. I was getting more comfortable knowing that nobody would kill me in front of the *staff*, which gave me a wisp of confidence.

The woman was standing at the door to the dining room, and I followed her as we entered a large room I could only describe as a reading room. It had some of the most amazing period furniture. Each piece belonged in a museum or behind a glass case in a billionaire's house. The walls had many fine paintings that were clearly masterpieces. It was all too much to take in at one time.

I stood there staring at the paintings, furniture, handblown glass pieces, sculptures, ceramics, and leather-bound books. The opulence completely overwhelmed me. Like the other rooms, oil lamps provided the light. I had to say, "Forgive me for asking, but are these all real?"

Another slight smile and a barely perceptible nod. My jaw must have been dragging on the floor. I was about to walk over to look at a piece of art, then thought better of it. Instead, I turned to the woman and asked softly, "May I?"

Another slight smile and barely perceptible nod. I inspected the nearest paintings, and it was exquisite. Every brushstroke, shadow, and face was perfect. I am not an art expert, but I knew these paintings were flawless. Even the frames were of the best quality—solid brass or hand-engraved silver. She had pottery from China, France, and Spain; statues of every type; carved glass; Egyptian art; Roman art; Russian art; and modern art.

All the pieces were flawless—no restoration. I saw signatures: Picasso, Monet, Dali, and Vermeer. As I studied a particularly stunning Rembrandt, I realized that the subject matter was a woman who looked like my captor. But, of course, this could not be my captor; Rembrandt had died long ago. I turned to look at the woman and saw another slight smile and a barely perceptible nod. *What did this mean? Did Rembrandt paint her? Was this her great-grandmother?*

The woman said in a far-off voice, "Yes, that is me in the painting. I still have the dress I wore in the picture."

I did not know how to react to the woman's statement. It must be a modern "made to look old" painting, but the quality was impeccable. It *had* to be a replica. Then I wondered all kinds of crazy thoughts. *Time travel? That might explain the missing razor and dining room cleanup. But that is not possible. Game show? Now we are on track, but what kind of track? Who would go to all this effort to make a painting like this?*

I decided the most likely scenario was a new big-budget reality television program. This explanation covered all the bases; there was probably a big prize in it for me. *This might be the exposure I need to get my career jump-started to the next level.* I started to get excited, but I realized the woman was scowling.

"Sorry," I stammered.

That admission took the scowl away. The woman motioned me to the sofa and said firmly, "We will talk now."

I walked over to a sofa that probably cost a hundred grand and asked, "Is this all right?"

Another slight smile. I quietly sat and then stared at the woman. There was an awkward silence for a long moment, and my eyes fixed on an immaculate set of cut-glass containers. Finally, she cleared her throat, then said in a serious tone, "I need you to be honest with me. It will save time, save you pain, and may even save your life."

I did not understand this basic request. Nobody had ever spoken so direct to me. I was back to square one. *What am I going to do? How is this going to play out? How much more pain will she inflict on me? What did she mean when she said, "save your life?"*

The woman's expression commanded an immediate answer. However, I did not know what to say, so I nodded. She was not pleased. "I need you to clearly convey your intent," she said.

This statement threw me into another panic, and I still did not know what to say. *Who could know how to answer this? Should I say "yes, yes"?* The woman started to speak again, but I interrupted, "I'll be as honest as I can be under these circumstances."

Another scowl. "Not a promising start," the woman chided. "You need to listen better and think before you speak. Please answer my question."

I closed my eyes. *What does this woman want? What is the magic answer that will gain my freedom? Will I ever see another sunset?* I told myself to focus. *Think, think, think! What does she want to hear?* I opened my eyes, stared directly at her, and confessed, "I'm sorry, but the gravity of your question caught me off guard. I'll put all of my efforts into being honest and respectful of your needs."

I did not know if the word "respectful" worked, but I knew this answer could make or break me. Then she shot me another piercing stare, and a huge chill shot up my spine. *How is she doing this chill-ray mental-stare thing?* I continued to be frightened, but the voice in my head told me to man up. I stared right back at her, imagining daggers shooting out of my eyes. My effort did not work. I felt as if I were still a little boy trying to answer a math question in front of the class, and I did not know what two plus two equaled. It then dawned on me that my fear was winning.

I kept wondering, *What does she want?* Finally, I had an inkling of an idea. I took my free hand and folded it over my restrained hand to show some dignity. Then, I tilted my head up slightly, and with as much calm as I could muster, I thought, *I will give honest and direct answers.* I repeated this in my mind over and over and tried to block out all my fearful thoughts. Finally, my chill lessened and the woman's stare grew less ominous. She folded her arms without breaking her stare and then said, "All right."

The woman sat back and asked calmly, "How do your hands feel?"

That question jolted me back to reality. I became aware that I needed to breathe, and a cold sweat drenched me. Time had passed, but I was unaware of how much. The woman asked again, this time more loudly, "How do your hands feel?"

I saw a flash of impatience in the woman's expression. I knew I needed to answer quickly and was about to mutter "fine," but I stopped myself. *This was a test.* I thought while wondering out how she wanted me to answer her.

I composed myself, gave my situation some thought, and wiggled my fingers to test their movement. Then, with the most amount of confidence I could muster, I answered, "I'm sorry I didn't answer sooner."

Another nod and I continued, "My hands are painful and numb. My wrist took much of the fall, and there may be a bruise."

"Can you type or hold a pen well enough for writing?" the woman asked.

So, this was it. She wanted me to rewrite one of my books. I was about to blurt out "yes," but paused. I knew I needed to use a pen for writing notes. The woman looked at me for a long moment and said, "I did not plan your fall."

The woman motioned me up, then un-cuffed my bound hand. She stared hard and said with great confidence, "No tricks. You are not fast enough."

The woman handed me a piece of aged paper and a nice pen. I wrote out the alphabet and the sentence: "This is a complete test of my handwriting ability."

My hands hurt, but I could write. I composed my thoughts and murmured, "My hands are stiff, but with some effort, I can write with breaks every so often."

This answer seemed to please the woman. I then noticed that the faded paper had the letterhead of the Savoy Hotel in London. The upper corner was dated 1886. Another mystery.

The woman folded her slim hands, looked down at them, and seemed to ponder something deep. She looked up for a long moment and then nodded. I could not read the woman's expression, but she seemed to be facing a deep dilemma.

The woman talked slowly and carefully, in a tone she had not used before, "I went to great lengths to select you. I would wish that you would write . . . about my life. I promise it will be an interesting story."

The woman again looked at her hands and moved them uncomfortably, but the voice in my head screamed, "Don't say a word!" Inside, I was confused and excited. Did she really want me to write her biography? Could it be that simple? I patiently waited and took great care to keep an open mind. Finally, the woman again spoke in a quiet, reserved voice. "I had tried over the years to capture my own story. The results were . . . unflattering. I decided it would be best to have some-body else write my story. This will be an arduous process, as I never speak about myself—my real self."

This admission completely floored me. *All the dying, torture, ex-wife, book-altering theories were wrong, and I might actually survive this ordeal.* I did not know what to say because she had not posed a question. So I went with something neutral, "I understand. Thank you for sharing your motives with me."

This statement seemed to brighten the woman up slightly. Then she turned serious again and asked with a piercing stare, "Can you do this?"

A chill hit me deep in my abdomen, and it instantly brought back a memory. When I was five, I put a fork in the electric toaster and got the shock of my life. My mother pulled me away; I nearly died. This piercing sensation felt similar, and I knew I was at a disadvantage. I fought back the demons and concentrated on the question. *Can I do this? Can I do this?*

It suddenly occurred to me that I had a choice. I could get out of this situation. With this in mind, I asked, "What if I cannot?"

As soon as the words left my mouth, I regretted asking. The woman seemed confused, but she instantly composed herself and demanded, "Answer my question! Can you do this?"

I knew I could pen a simple biography. What I wanted was to get out of danger. I looked into the woman's eyes and saw something new. She was *asking* me to capture her story. This was not a demand but an honest, humble request. I could tell I had upset her by bringing up the possibility I might not fulfill her request, and I felt ashamed.

With great care, I composed the best answer that I could: "As you know, my background is in writing fiction. But, in college, I wrote four biographies as class assignments. For one, I interviewed a local politician. I got mostly Bs in this effort. Nevertheless, I'm confident I have the knowledge and experience to capture your story."

I did not think my answer satisfied the woman. She continued to stare, but I was not as intimidated this time. I no longer fought back and instead, I opened myself up to her stare. I had not lied; I had stated the facts as I understood them to be. There was silence for a long time. The woman again looked at her hands and fidgeted. I took a deep breath and turned away.

Then my mind drifted. *Is she telepathic or an alien? What is this arrow-throwing-eyes, chilling-staring trick? Can I even write her story? Is that really her in the painting?* I stole another look at the painting. It looked like her. I needed to take over this conversation, so I stood up and stretched my arms. About four joints popped, and then I sat down again. I gave the woman a somewhat confident, questioning look. Her expression changed to being slightly angry. I think she realized I had broken her one-sided concentration game. The woman looked down at her hands again and then looked back at me harshly. Finally, she asked with a curious, pleading voice, "Will you?"

Her direct request hit me like a brick. I knew I had to be strong, and I needed to make this eye staring dagger intimidation go my way, but the chills shot through me. I felt dizzy, and my head hurt. I did not know what to say, and I felt I was losing my life force (whatever that was). So I closed my eyes, composed myself, and thought about her request.

A big issue was that I did not understand the consequences of declining her request. My best guess was that she would kill me if I did not comply. This was because she had said that giving her honest answers could save my life. However, the prospect of spending time learning her story was unsettling.

When I opened my eyes, I could tell that capturing her story was *really* important to her. I felt that, as a writer, I had responsibilities. This was a strange, new feeling, and I wondered where it came from. I also wondered why capturing her story was so important.

It then occurred to me that this was my big opportunity to do something great. While I was not entirely committed, I decided I would indeed be the person to capture her story. Therefore, I spoke in my best calm voice as I responded, "Yes, of course."

I returned the woman's stare with all of my energy, keeping the chill from completely taking over my mind. After some time, she sat back, and I realized she had been holding her breath. It dawned on me that she was not all-powerful and that this effort was also hard for her. I began to feel more confident and tried even harder to stare right back.

The uplifting feeling did not last. The woman looked back at me, nodded slightly, and declared, "At this point, you cannot possibly understand what you committed yourself to. I have decided to proceed, and there will be no turning back—for you or me."

I felt like when I would click "accept" on one of those impossibly long computer legal forms while not knowing what I was agreeing to. The woman summed up our conversation by reaffirming, "You are committed."

The woman looked down at her hands, but the chill did not go away. Her action made me realized I was in far over my head.

The silence was upsetting, and I needed to make a positive gesture by asking in a gentlemanly tone, "Would you like some tea? I think a beverage would complement our breakthrough."

The woman shot me a questioning look, then quietly left the room. She returned with an exquisite silver tray with a stainless steel teapot and several small baked items. I offered to pour the tea, but she stopped me. "It must steep for at least six and a half minutes. Please try a hibiscus-almond macaroon."

I took a small plate, an exquisitely embroidered mini napkin, and one of the elegant baked goods. The fantastic taste again surprised me. *How could something so good even exist? Bear fat instead of butter, or an alien food maker?* Either way, the delicious flavor was beyond me. I made an attempt at seeing where this biography effort was going and stammered, "How would you like to begin? We could start with some basic background information."

As soon as my words came out, I knew that, in my haste, I had completely botched it. The woman's icy stare returned. I realized she had probably thought about this for a long time and knew exactly how she wanted to proceed. I felt a good scolding coming, a quick jab to the ribs, or even my hands back in restraints.

I went for broke by asserting myself with as much confidence as I could gather and said, "This will not work. I'm not a mind reader like you, and I clearly don't have your experience level. I was trying to convey my interest in the project."

The woman was taken aback but quickly regained her composure. She forced a smile and sidestepped my last statement, "The tea smells ready."

It had not been six and a half minutes, but she poured the tea. I took a sip, and of course, it was the best I had ever had. So I gave the best smile, and in my best cheerful voice, I said, "This is great tea. What kind is it?"

Another expression I could not read crossed the woman's face, then she looked into her cup and began a serious discourse as if she were teaching a child. "This strain is called White Darjeeling, and it was a personal favorite of Mahatma Gandhi's. His good friend Laalamani grew this tea on an east-facing hillside with minimal water. He used volcanic soil mixed with special clay to make this batch. It was grown in the fall of 1911 and has become even better with age. Laalamani was nice enough to give me a portion, and I use it for important occasions."

Wow, blow me off the face of the earth! Again, a million questions. *You knew Gandhi? Does this explain the painting? How's this possible? Are you a time traveler? Are we going to go back in time to meet Laalamani?* I almost asked, but she held up her hand as if to stop my silly thoughts and said, "You have many questions. I will answer them in time.

First, you must understand me and what I am. Words cannot describe this experience."

Okay, a million questions are up in smoke. I wanted to be diplomatic and encouraged her by asking, "How may I help?"

I could not read the woman's expression, and she went on to say, "You will not appreciate what comes next. You will need more courage than you have ever applied before. You must do your best to be strong."

I was again frightened beyond description and made one last attempt at basic conversation, "May I at least know your name?"

This time, I got a genuine smile but no name.

FOUR

The woman stood up from the sofa and motioned for me to get up. She gestured toward a door that appeared to lead outside. At the door, the woman stopped me by placing her hand on my chest. She quietly grasped my hands and then buckled them into their restraints. I noticed something different in the woman's facial expression. Her eyes held a sad or painful memory. She positioned herself behind me and, for the first time, spoke in a quiet, unsure voice, "I allow you to turn back."

Of course, I wanted to turn back. *Let me go! Please! I am begging you!* My mind demanded. However, the voice in my head had other ideas. It screamed that I had to do this. After thinking for a moment, I raised my head, turned around, and composed myself. I then assured her in my most confident voice, "I should see your request through. I made a commitment."

I looked at the woman, and tears began forming. The prospect of something so horrible that it brought tears was beyond frightening. She let out a long sigh and motioned me forward. I did not know if the woman was testing me or not. I began realizing the gravity of passing up my one chance to stop whatever insanity was about to occur.

We stepped out into a well-maintained yard. I noticed a barn with what appeared to be farm implements on my left. I looked at several rows of trees, a huge garden, and a greenhouse in front of me. The landscaping was immaculate, and I could not spot a single weed.

The air smelled refreshing, and the sun felt invigorating. A nearby porch on my right had a cozy area with a small stack of books next to a nice reading chair. On the side of the house sat a huge, white propane tank on a large trailer. I was staring at it, the woman noticed, and she said, "That's for the refrigerator."

Wait a minute. I thought. *Propane equals fire, which equals cold?* Her statement made little sense. We continued walking, and I saw a well-maintained flower garden, enormous cedar trees, bushes loaded with blackberries, and an exercise area. "Wow, quite a nice spread you have here," I commented. "You turned this beautiful landscape into a cozy living area."

I did not get a response, and we kept walking. On the other side of the house was a row of cars, including my car. The other cars were a mix of new, nice, old, crashed, and junked. She parked the tow truck at the end. To me, this sight was a parking lot full of red flags. I wanted to ask about them, but thought it would be safer not to.

We took a three-foot-wide, well-worn path into the woods. There were rut marks from a cart or trailer. It was muddy, but I managed despite the foot restraints. I began seeing reluctance in her movements, and this display of emotion frightened me even further. The path eventually opened up to a flat clearing. In the center was a gruesome sight: four rusty iron cages, and two of them contained men!

When the men looked at us, they became deeply terrified. I did not understand why they were not screaming until I noticed their mouths had tape over them. She bound their limbs inside locked cages. Their clothes were in tatters, and their bodies had many bleeding bruises. The men were filthy and showed signs of having been there for a while. It was not clear if the cuts were self-inflicted or not. When our eyes met, I could see they were frightened, but I could not tell if their fear was of the woman or me. It hit me once again that, despite this woman's promise, I might not live through this!

In the center of the clearing was a menacing-looking, well-used table with an indentation at the one end. Next to the table was a large tool chest with several drawers, all covered in clear plastic. Two carts looked like they might have been used to carry bodies. Strangely, there was a kind of doctor's chair with mirrors. It made little sense. Ominously, I noticed a big wooden post near the table with rings on it. I did not know its purpose, but this sight scared me the most.

My legs buckled, and I started to scream, but the woman's voice broke my instinct, "Quiet, or I will tape your mouth shut!"

I stopped yelling and began crying. She moved me toward the post and began saying in a kind voice, "James . . . James . . . you will not die. Try to stay strong."

This statement did not help. My sinuses opened up, and I dribbling mucus. My eyes streamed tears, and I was making huge, desperate, crying sobs. I had never been so scared and out of control. Finally, I forced myself to look down at the ground. The woman must have noticed my aversion, and she said, "We will wait a minute."

I did not know if the woman was taking pity on me or not. Some amount of time later, she said in a commanding tone, "This is important. You must observe everything you see. Later, you must repeat every step yourself. Your life now depends on your ability to observe and remember. Stay focused, ignore the unpleasant images, and record in your mind what is happening."

I did not know how to process this enormous amount of information. *Whatever did she mean? What was I going to record and repeat?* Unfortunately, instead of concentrating, I turned inward and focused on how pitiful I was.

The woman gave me another minute to recover, then decided it was time to proceed. She was still holding me by my restraining belt, and her powerful muscles prevented me from running away. The woman tied me to a chair made out of recently cut logs that faced the men in the cages.

Suddenly, the woman splashed cold water on my face. I jerked from the shock and then looked up. She had removed the plastic from the toolbox, and she took out what looked like surgical instruments. The woman wore a stained, black-leather apron. She also had a thin, clear face mask like a dentist would use. For some reason, my mind briefly wandered, and I wondered if my dentist shopped at the same face mask store.

The two men in the cages looked horrified and started wrenching themselves about. I wondered what was going to happen next and if the two men knew. The woman cleaned leaves off the doctor's chair and positioned the mirrors to her liking. She then stared at all she had done. It looked like she was trying to determine whether she had forgotten anything.

The woman turned to me with an angry expression that commanded my attention. She took a well-worn notebook from one of the tool chest drawers, coughed slightly, consulted the notebook, and began in a loud voice, "James, remember you will not die. Pull yourself together! This is important! Pay attention! Pay attention!"

After consulting her notebook, she continued in a loud voice, "This man's name is Gerald Donner, and he is an abuser of our society."

The woman glared at me and again yelled, "Pay attention!" Then she pinched my arm, glared again, and continued, "This man seduces women with drugs, has sex with them, and then takes compromising pictures. He then blackmails them with the pictures. Often his demand is for more sex. Even if they comply, he sends the pictures to their work and family for spite. Three women took their own lives rather than submit to his demands."

Gerald's green eyes were wide, and all the color had gone out of his skin. *What was she going to say about the other man? What was she going to say about me? Did she get all this information from her icy staring trick? Did she torture him to get this information? What was Gerald's side of the story?* I thought in complete confusion.

The woman went over to the toolbox and retrieved a brass tool. She adjusted a knob on the tool and then used a wooden match to ignite a flame near its tip. A minute later, the woman adjusted the flame, making it smaller. She then brought the tool over to the man and burned his belly. Gerald immediately recoiled to the side of the cage in pain. This sight shocked me beyond belief. *How could she burn a living person with no emotion?* I thought in horror.

Gerald tried to scream, but the tape prevented it. The loud whistling noise from his nose breathing was extreme. Finally, the woman commanded, "I am now going to 'harvest' you. You will die so that we may live."

Gerald was trying to make himself as small as he could against the corner of the cage, and the woman applied the hot tip to his side. I could smell the smoke of his burning flesh.

Suddenly, it occurred to me that the woman had used the word "we." *How will I be involved in all of this? What will she do with me? What was my role? Was she going to make me eat Gerald's burned flesh?* That cannibalistic thought heightened my terror.

The woman burned him two more times in the belly. Gerald was exhausted, but I still saw his extreme anger and fear. It was then that I realized she burned Gerald to obtain the maximum level of pain. The woman continued burning and glaring at him until a point when she smiled thinly.

Suddenly, with a lightning-quick movement, the woman hit Gerald on the temple. It took me a second to realize that she had been holding a hammer with an elongated narrow head that allowed her to strike him right through the cage. Gerald slumped to the side, and his body twitched.

Seeing Gerald's body position made me cry out. The woman turned to me with a face devoid of expression and said, in a calm voice, "James. He is not dead. However, he will soon pass. Therefore, we must act quickly."

The woman's calm words and casual attitude shocked me to my core. There was absolutely no remorse. *Who was she?* Suddenly it hit me again. The woman again used the word "we." *What did I have to do with all of this? Why am I here?*

The woman unlatched the cage and dragged out the body. Then, hefting him easily, she flopped him up on the table, face-down. *How could a woman of medium build move a big, heavy body with one arm?* It was then that I noticed the table end was intended for a head to fit into. The woman then turned to me and undid the restraints that were holding me in the chair. I stood up, and she said directly to me, "You will pay close attention. Do you understand?"

It occurred to me that the woman was yelling over my uncontrollable sobs, and I nodded. She grabbed my hair, pointed my face toward the body, and yelled, "Pay close attention!"

Once satisfied I was looking in the right direction, the woman picked up a scalpel from the tray of instruments. She made a quick, deep incision in his left lower back, parallel to his ribs. To my surprise, there was less than a drop of blood. I could not believe the precise hand dexterity she commanded. It then dawned on me that she had cut into a living person witch further horrified me.

41

The woman used a spoon-like instrument to reach into the incision and cut with a different, smaller scalpel. She took something bloody out of Gerald's back and then placed it in a small teacup. The woman smiled and said in a confident tone, "This is the pancreas. Look at the color. It is healthy and will do nicely."

Although the woman spoke with a pleasant smile, her words still repulsed beyond comprehension. I was hoping the gore was over, but she quickly made another incision and used the spoon-like tool to remove something. While working, she spoke in an authoritative voice, "I've extracted the left and right adrenal glands. Normally I only extract the left, but you are here."

This casual statement took me to a new level of horror. *What did I have to do with this? Was she going to force me to eat Gerald's organs?*

The woman glared at me and said, "Applying pain to Gerald stimulated the adrenal gland to make fresh adrenaline and the steroid aldosterone. So I need a section of the kidney."

The woman reached in through the second incision and removed another bloody mass. There were now four teacups filled with Gerald's body parts. During her work, she kept saying, "Pay attention!" and I lost count of the number of times she repeated this phrase.

The whole gory procedure had taken less than five minutes. As I looked, the body was still twitching and obviously alive. Finally, the woman looked at me and solemnly stated, "He will not survive. I will now put him down; he will feel no pain."

The woman took a V-shaped knife and made a quick jab into the base of his skull. I presumed that the man known as Gerald was now dead.

The experience left me deflated, weak, confused, and tired. I desperately wanted to leave the wooded area. The body still twitched, but now in a slow, withering way. This sight made me want to throw up.

Gerald was dead. Nobody could survive a cut like that to the neck. Was it still possible that this was a TV show? Could they use computer graphics to create all of this? Was she going to make me eat his body parts? As my mind screamed for answers, I noticed that the man in the other cage was going wild and wrenching back and forth against his restraints.

Again, the woman commanded my attention by pulling my hair and said, "Now for the hard part. Look closely!"

There was something that was harder than watching her torture and kill a man? What incarnation of mutilation could possibly come next? This thought mortified me. The woman took the last teacup with the kidney section, added a liquid to it from an ornate vessel, and said, "This is mint oil. Watch how I am doing this. See how the liquid changes color?"

The woman worked the mint oil against the kidney in a circular motion with two blue sticks with pincushion-like ends. Soon the mint liquid took on a brown, then slightly gray tint. There were about ten drops. The woman then took one of the two cups with the adrenal glands and gently squeezed one gland with a round black stick and a second V-shaped stick. This produced about five drops of bloody liquid. She repeated this with the second adrenal gland in another cup. My terror briefly subsided as I became curious about the sight before me. *How did she figure this out? What was the meaning of this?* So much was going on in my mind.

The woman walked over to a small box I had not noticed before and opened it with great care. In a flash, she put her hand in and retrieved a black snake. It writhed around her hand, and was clearly upset at being disturbed. *Was the snake for the other person in the cage? Was it for me? Was I going to die from a snakebite?*

The woman decisively picked up the teacup containing the adrenal gland liquid with the other. She forced the snake's mouth open and held it in such a way that one fang touched the lip of the cup. The woman placed that cup down and repeated the procedure with the other cup containing the liquid from the adrenal gland. She then placed the snake back in the box. The woman stared at the snake, smiled, and said in a soothing tone, "That's a good boy, Alfred. Thank you again for your contribution. I'll get you a nice fat rat later today."

For a second, I thought the woman was going to kiss the snake. She then gently put Alfred back in his box. The woman turned to me and said calmly, "Alfred is an African cobra. His venom works better than the Egyptian cobra's. Notice how I use less than a drop. This is all that is necessary."

The woman then carefully stirred the snake venom liquid in the teacups with a slender black stick. She showed me the liquid, and to my surprise, it had congealed like Jell-O. The woman then stirred the mint liquid with another black stick. Carefully, she mixed the kidney-mint liquid and the snake venom-adrenal liquid together in one cup. The woman then did this same procedure with the other cup. Finally, she showed me the mixed liquid; it formed a gooey, yellow-pink paste. The woman then turned her attention to the pancreas and cut it into two pieces, using a pair of small golden scissors.

With a relieved look on her face, the woman said, "I'm going to go first."

I did not know what "going first" meant. *What was she going to do? What was going on?* The woman placed the pancreas, and the cup of mixed liquid on a ceramic plate made for this purpose.

The woman moved to the doctor's chair and got into it backward. Despite the restraints, I moved my body to face her. The chair appeared to accommodate her well. She looked at me, gave me an intense stare, and stated, "This mirror is necessary for when you have to do this procedure to yourself. You must pay close attention."

What did she mean when she said, ". . . when you have to do this procedure yourself?" *What was I going to do to myself?* I wanted to run away, but I found myself riveted by the process being shown to me. She adjusted the mirrors and pulled back her shirt to reveal a small, healed, one-and-a-half-inch incision near her neck and right shoulder blade. This was a completely different location from where Gerald's organs were removed, and I did not understand the significance of this incision.

The woman adjusted the mirrors to ensure that she could view the right shoulder blade perfectly. Then, without looking at me, she again told me to pay attention. The woman then used a scalpel to open up her incision. It surprised me to see how little blood came out, and this demonstration of skill made it clear she had done this procedure many times. I should have been horrified, but I found it fascinating.

The woman got a copper spoon, inserted the spoon into her incision, and removed something. She placed this item on the ceramic tray off to one side. The woman then used a different copper spoon to take the prepared pancreas out of its cup and, to my horror, put it inside her incision. She then took a small, black stick and dipped it into the teacup containing the liquid I had watched her prepare. The woman applied this liquid to the inside of the incision. She then used a small curved needle and quickly made two small sutures.

As a finishing touch, the woman applied antiseptic and a small bandage. It amazed me that she did not spill a drop of blood. She pulled her shirt back into place. It had taken her less than two minutes to do whatever the heck she had done.

The woman got up, steadied herself, and seemed to be fine. Then, she flashed a wicked smile, and said, "Your turn."

I stammered, "Wait, wait . . ."

The woman undid my restraints, grabbed me, tossed Gerald down on the ground, and threw me on the table with a quick flick of her wrist. Then, out of nowhere came a strap to hold me down.

No, no, this couldn't be happening! Was she going to put that thing inside of me? Then, to my horror, I realized my face was in the same hole that Gerald had just been in. My imagination told me it was still warm, and I swear I smelled his sweat.

The woman pulled down my shirt, revealing my shoulder. Quickly, she cut deeply into my right shoulder in the same place where she had her incision. This action should have caused great pain, but it felt cold. I screamed anyway.

I could see the woman scoop up the pancreas with the copper spoon and put it in me. She applied the fluid with the black stick and then made two small sutures. Finally, she applied a bandage and antiseptic over the wound. It stunned me that in less than two minutes, it was all done. *What was all done? Had she actually put that thing in me? Do I have snake venom inside my body? Am I going to die?*

I was still crying when the woman took off the straps to let me up. I looked at her, and she had a joyful expression. She let me sit on a log as she cleaned the instruments, plates, and cups with alcohol. I continued to cry, and my shoulder began hurting. I stared at the person in the other cage. He looked deflated, and I could see tears and mucus running down his face.

We started back toward the house, and the woman complimented me, sounding thoughtful. "You handled that better than I thought you would."

With a defeated, empty voice, I replied, "I feel horrible. Did that man have to die?"

The woman looked at me and smiled. It was hard to understand why she would be happy about killing a man and putting snake venom in me. The woman put both of my arms in the restraint, and as we walked, she began holding my arm, like we were on some sort of first date. It was so crazy. *Was this how she got off? Was I some sort of boy toy to her?* One minute the woman was jabbing me in the solar plexus to inflict pain, and the next minute she was holding my arm like we were gathering flowers. *Who's this woman? Why me?* I did not know what to think.

At the house, we stopped at the porch, and the woman motioned for me to sit down. She took off my leg restraints and then removed my arm restraints. She looked at me with thoughtful eyes and said sympathetically, "You have been through a lot. I'll bring some refreshments."

I did not know how to respond; my mind was in a fog. I mumbled, "How do you know I won't run away?"

The woman formed a slight smirk and answered, "You will not run."

I did not know what to make of that statement. When the woman went inside, I stood up—and then sat right back down. Now I knew what she meant. I had no strength, and my head spun when I tried to stand. A few minutes later, she came out with a silver tray holding two glasses and a pitcher. I noticed an intricate, etched pattern. The theme was a herd of deer that ran from one glass to the next. I suspected they were Italian.

Why was I trying to guess who made the glasses at a time like this? A man was killed, and his bloody body parts were in my now-painful shoulder. Inside the pitcher was a light-brown liquid with some kind of fresh leaves. The woman poured some liquid into each glass, and I took a sip. It tasted wonderful and refreshing. I started feeling better, and she immediately poured me another glass with a smile.

I asked the woman what it was, and she answered, "This is a drink my mother and I used to enjoy. It is birch tree bark tea with fresh mint and lemon. I've improved on my mother's recipe by adding agave from the Mexican state of Coahuila."

This was one more element I did not know how to process, but the taste was amazing. The woman only had one sip, but I finished off the pitcher. I collected my thoughts, and asked, "Do I get to know your name?"

This made the woman smirk, and she got a far-off look for a long moment. "I've gone by so many names," she answered. "The name I use now came from a child who died shortly after birth. Barbara Edwards. Do you like that name? I think it sounds refined. If you asked me my name, I would answer Miss Edwards. Always Miss. But the name I was born with . . . well, I have not used that name in a long time. Hmm . . . you have got me looking at my hands. It is a compulsive habit that I only do when I am deep in thought."

Barbara looked at me with a kind smile and continued in a soft voice, "My given name is Anitchka. The English translation of this is 'Grace.' My family name is Ermolaev. Anitchka Ermolaev. Saying this name out loud brings back many memories. For our conversations, you may call me Grace. Yes, that is appropriate."

Learning Grace's name floored me. I felt as though I finally had the first piece of the puzzle. We sat for a moment, and I could finally relax slightly. Then, she gestured to the trees, which were blowing in a slight breeze, and asked in a whimsical voice, "Beautiful, yes?"

I nodded, and we sat in silence for a long moment. Finally, Grace said in a kind voice, "I'll tell you one piece of information about me, and then you will rest until morning."

I shifted my head a bit in Grace's direction to show interest. However, I now knew my body was not well. I realized I felt nauseous, and my head felt like it was floating in mud. She again looked at her hands, then off into the distance, and for the first time, spoke to me without her direct, piercing eyes.

"I was born sixty-five kilometers east of the small town of Valdai in what people now call Russia. The house that I grew up in has long since fallen into disrepair. The only thing recognizable from our house is the apple tree that my father and I planted. It is still a sturdy tree, and I visit it every few years to pay my family respects. You would like the taste of its fruit. It is strong and sweet. My mother told me I was born on that very spot, which is why my father and I planted the apple tree there. The part of this story that you would find of interest is the year in which my birth occurred; it was 1498. As it is 2012, I am 514 years old."

What was this? This was not possible! I had so many questions and stammered, "Is this like . . ."

Grace cut me off with a gesture of her hand and said in a commanding voice, "You must rest; tomorrow will be another big day."

I had to ask, "Is this like the movie *Highlander?*"

Grace looked a question mark at me, and I blurted out, "You know, the movie where you can live forever if you kill the other immortal guys, and *there can only be one?*"

Grace replied in a disappointed voice, "I do not know of this movie. You should concentrate on reality. We do not live in movie fantasy."

FIVE

Grace guided me inside and led me to the bathroom. She handed me some clothing. "This should fit you. Clean yourself and leave your clothing here. Do not get your incision wet."

Grace stared at me for a moment, then walked away. I obediently took the bundle of clothing into the bathroom and noticed that there was a bathtub. I had not realized that large object before. *Was this the same bathroom?* So I stripped off my clothes and turned on the water to draw a bath.

I looked at the clothing and saw mucus all over my shirt. With all my sobbing, I probably drained out a lifetime of snot. Looking at the mess, I felt like a vagrant and wanted to say: *I'm not a child. I had to cry. It was not my fault! I'm really a man!*

A moment later, the water in the tub looked ready. I noticed a small dish with soap and a glass container that held what appeared to be shampoo. As soon as I got in, the warm water relaxed me. As I soaked, I reflected on all that had occurred. Finally, my little voice told me to put everything aside and concentrate on being alive.

Carefully, I felt the incision. It hurt when I touched it, but otherwise, it seemed fine. I thought about opening the incision and digging out what she had put in. I knew there was deadly cobra venom in my body that should kill me, but I found myself trusting her. *Wait, did I really trust her?*

I picked up the soap, let it lather a bit, and applied it to my face. It smelled wonderful and felt even better. *Why is everything here the best I have ever had? Why does the soap have to smell fantastic?* The soap was not good or great. The soap smelled absolutely *perfect.* This simple smell confused me even further.

I turned on the tap, made a cup with my hand, and tasted the water. Of course—the best water I have ever had. *Magic mountain spring water?* I smelled the liquid in the shampoo bottle and then applied it to my head. It did not surprise me it lathered up wonderfully and made my scalp tingle.

I sat in the tub and contemplated what had been going on before washing up and rinsing off. I had forgotten to check for a towel before starting the bath, but a luxurious, embroidered red cotton towel was neatly folded next to the sink. Again, the softest towel I had ever used.

I tried to think of an explanation for all I had been experiencing. *Was this a dream or a virtual reality computer simulation? Was I even alive? Was it still possible that this was a reality television show? No,* I decided, *that man really died, and my situation was not a television show.*

My nighttime clothing was unique. The best description would be executive-gray sleeping garment meets old-time England pajamas. The fine linen or silk fabric had remarkable embroidery in a striped theme. The seams were absolutely perfect. I felt like a king wearing it, which lifted my spirits. *Where did she buy this garment? Is there a store for this kind of clothing? SleepingGearForKings.com?*

I was still having trouble standing and had to steady myself against the walls. While moving, I tried not to leave finger-prints. I gathered my dirty clothes, hung up the towel, and opened the door. I expected to see Grace crossing her arms and pointing at something, but there was only an empty hallway, dimly lit with an oil lamp. I did not understand why her not being there was a letdown.

I walked through the hallway and made my way to the kitchen. Grace was there, wearing a custom-fit apron, and she was cooking. *How can a cooking apron be custom-fit?* She motioned toward the table, and I put my clothes there.

Grace was making dough, and there was a pot on the stove. The smell was intoxicating. She took a quick glance at me, turned back to her cooking, and said quietly, "Those nightclothes suit you. Please get some rest. You must not disturb your incision."

I thought for a moment and asked humbly, "May I ask what time it is?"

Without looking up, Grace answered, "I do not have a clock in this room, but judging by the sun's shadow, it is approxi-mately 12:15 in the afternoon. You must rest."

I was about to ask about restraints or what would happen if I tried to leave, but I was too tired. I hobbled away toward the bedroom. When I got to the bedroom, I noticed the bed restraints were no longer present. I got under the covers and relaxed. I wanted to figure out how to get out of my situation, but I fell asleep even before my head hit the pillow.

I startled myself awake out of a nightmare. There were five "Grace-looking" women in different crazy outfits, all stabbing me with knives.

I tried to sit up and went right back down. My body told me that there was a big problem. If I were at home, I would have called 911 and made the paramedics drive me to the nearest emergency room with sirens blaring. My body felt like it was fighting something and losing badly. Nausea made it hard to think, and I decided to touch my wound, but I could not make my arms work properly. It took some time to coordinate my movements, but eventually, I felt it.

My wound hurt, but not as much as I would have expected. I looked at the corner of the room and saw a neat pile of clothes. I fell out of bed and crawled over to the pile. While lying on the floor, I changed into my new outfit. It was a crazy mix of black pants, a blue shirt, and a red undershirt. The style was a distinguished, '80s MTV-music-video-DJ meets old-time-European gentleman.

It took ten minutes, but I stood up and look into a small mirror on the wall. I did not recognize the face staring back at me. Somehow, I thought I looked younger. I knew that could not be the case, but the mirror also told me that my new clothes made me look elegant and presentable. I concluded that the fine clothes just made me look younger, perhaps even more hip. I had great trouble walking and slowly hobbled to the hallway.

The kitchen was empty, and I noticed the butcher block had fifteen knives. It occurred to me that I could easily conceal one. However, I knew Grace would see a missing knife. So I walked toward the dining room. She set the table for two, but there was no food present.

I had to steady myself for another minute and went into the next room. I found Grace sitting on the sofa reading. She looked up and asked quietly, "Do you like the poems of Machado?"

"Who?"

Grace asked again, "In college, did you study Antonio Machado?"

It took a lot of focus for me to mumble a reply, "I'm not familiar with his work."

Grace looked back at her book, shook her head, and said in a slightly sarcastic voice, "The youth of today."

A minute later, Grace closed her book and stood up. She walked behind me and inspected my incision. Then, seemingly satisfied, Grace motioned for me to sit down. I collapsed on the sofa, and she sat down next to me, friendly once again.

Grace seemed deep in thought. She looked away from me as she said, "You have been through a tremendous experience. Today will be more difficult, and in the next two hours, you will feel dreadful. We will wait for the peak of this bad feeling to proceed. For now, you must eat and try not to hurt yourself while walking."

Grace's voice and demeanor had changed. She was more congenial, and I did not know why. Then, a strange thought occurred to me, *I had joined her club.* I found this profoundly unsettling.

I was full of questions and becoming aware that my body was getting worse. I had a terrible desire to do something, but

I did not know what it was. It took much effort, but I collected my thoughts and asked, "I need to ask, what is happ . . ."

Grace held up her hand, stopping my conversation in the middle of my words, and politely said, "You must eat. I will answer your questions when you are thinking clearly."

With that, Grace motioned me up and guided me to the dining room, where I sat. I stared without purpose at the empty table. Next, she brought out a small plate with pastries and a small glass of what appeared to be grape juice. These were placed where Grace had sat the previous evening. She then brought out a large bowl of whitish-yellowish goo and placed it in front of me.

Grace sat across from me and took a dainty bite of a pastry. I placed my napkin in my lap, which took a surprising amount of coordination and effort. I saw a single piece of silverware in front of me: a large spoon.

I took a scoop of the goo and ate it. Whatever it was tasted bland, but I continued to eat. Grace ate half of what was on her plate and seemed finished. She said, in a whimsical voice, "I'm sorry, but I already ate dinner, and I dislike eating between meals. I also must apologize for your meal. It is a Southern American dish called grits. Right now, this is what your body needs, and it will prevent you from feeling sick."

I still did not understand. *Had I slept for an afternoon, or a day, or a week?* I did not have my watch and wanted to ask about getting it back.

We returned to the study sofa room, where Grace picked up her book. My body and mind were getting worse. Everything hurt; I had mood swings, and I could not keep a single lucid thought. I had an intense headache, and the room was spinning. Grace briefly left the room, came back with a brass trash can in the shape of an elephant foot, and admonished me: "Try not to get sick, but if you do, use this."

I looked at the trash can and admired the exquisite metalwork. However, I could not focus on her words. The room was spinning more and more, but a kind of drive was building inside of me. I looked at Grace, and she was concentrating on her book. Every so often, her eyes darted toward me. I wanted to talk, but I could not form the words. She kept reading while my world was spinning out of control. A few minutes later, I thought I would vomit.

Grace finished her book, got up to look closely at me, and said, "Not long now. It is getting dark. I had hoped that we could do this during the light. How are you feeling?"

I mumbled something. Grace nodded and said, "Almost time. One hour, perhaps."

Grace opened a small, finely crafted wooden trunk and brought out a small wooden sewing hoop that secured a large piece of white linen fabric. She next brought out a picture of a hummingbird. Grace started sewing, occasionally looking up at me.

Sometime later, Grace came over and showed me what she had been working on. The hoop contained an intricate hummingbird embroidery. She sewed it to match the colors and pattern exactly. The thread she used had an impossible-to-describe translucent sheen to it. I looked at the hummingbird, and Grace smiled. Then she put her unfinished work and her materials back in the trunk.

I was absently looking at one of the many fine paintings when she said, "This thread product is new to me, and I am enjoying its results. However, I am not sure how it will stand the test of time, so I am doing a small project to test its aging."

I now had uncontrollable shakes, which pleased Grace. She smiled and said, "Not long now."

I wanted to understand how much time was passing, but I could not comprehend enough to guess. However, I began experiencing something in the back of my mind niggling at me. I did not know what this thought was, but I knew it was important. I needed a plan or a goal—or *something*.

I began thinking about the man in the other cage, and it occurred to me that I needed to speak to him. So I steadied myself, stood up, and slowly headed for the door. This made Grace smile, and I knew she was genuinely happy. Of course, Grace being happy was probably a bad thing, but at that moment, I did not care; I only knew I had to see the person.

Grace held my arm to keep me balanced. As we approached the door, she picked up a lantern and lit it. I noticed several black rubber boots near the door, and we each put on a pair. She handed me a light jacket and took one for herself. It was cold, but I was not in a state of mind to care.

We walked to the circle along the same path we had taken earlier. It might have been my imagination, but Grace may have been humming to herself. Nothing was making sense. *Why did I want to see this man?*

We came to the clearing, and I could see the man inside his cage. Our presence startled him. Grace had me sit on the log, and I stared at him blankly. He looked terrified and struggled against his restraints. However, I felt calm, and my focus had sharpened.

Grace took off the plastic from the tool chest, adjusted the mirrors on the chair, and set up a black metal tripod. Next, she lit lanterns around the clearing, so there was sufficient light. Grace then took what appeared to be a small video camera out of her coat pocket and set it on the tripod. Finally, she set up a battery-operated spotlight near the doctor's chair.

Grace then sat beside me and took my arm. I was still staring blankly at the man. "Would you like to speak to him?" she asked.

While I was trying to figure out an appropriate response, Grace brought out her notebook. She began speaking in a monotone voice. "Before us stands Richard MacAfern. Richard is a writer. His specialty is writing unauthorized biographies and tabloid articles. His outlandish stories have caused great pain for those he wrote about.

"On a personal level, he enjoys having relationships with young girls. He feels justified by referring to these encounters as 'relationships' rather than 'rape.' Richard always wears a mask, gloves, and a condom during these encounters to hide his identity. For being only forty-one years old, he has caused considerable suffering to his community."

Grace turned to me and solemnly said, "James, what you have not been aware of until now is that you were my second choice. Richard was my first. He is a better writer, but his greed and dishonesty were his ultimate downfall. Inside he is a weak man. He has no heart and could not focus. When I presented him with a harvest, he would not stop complaining.

After the harvest, he dug out the pancreas with his butter knife at the dining room table. I hope you are a better choice."

Grace closed her notebook. If I were behaving normally, this information would have prompted some reaction, not the least because she had insulted my writing ability. But I continued to stare at Richard. Finally, Grace asked softly, "Would you like to speak with Richard?"

I did not think I would be capable of speaking a single word, but I nodded. Grace walked over to the tripod and pressed a button on the camera. A small red light came on. She cleared her throat and said, "I am recording this video to ensure that you uphold your commitment. If you fail, I will present this video to the public, and the authorities will hold you accountable."

Grace reached into the cage and yanked the tape off Richard's mouth. He screamed, and she said, "You are a despicable example of humanity."

Grace then burned Richard with her flame tool, and he screamed. I do not remember her lighting the tool. Then for some unknown reason, this display of pain did not upset me. It was simply not important. Then, she asked Richard, "Are you sorry for all the pain you have caused?"

Richard stared at Grace with wide eyes but did not answer. "Do you have anything to say?" she asked.

Richard did not reply, but I had to ask, "Is what she said all true? Did you hurt those girls?"

Richard glared at me and answered with gritted teeth, "Hurt them? No! Never! What do you think I am? A monster? I am a great lover, and afterward, they all wanted more. They all wanted it! They all wanted me! You gotta help me, and my name isn't . . ."

Grace jabbed Richard again with the hot device and he screamed. "James, for your own protection, you should not know his real name," she said. "Please do not ask him for that information."

Grace looked at me, smiled, and said in an amused tone, "Notice the denial of evil. The bad ones embrace their villainous path. This one is not too special. I would give him a four out of ten. James, you are a two."

Was this a compliment or an insult? The statement barely registered with me. I continued to stare at the man known as Richard.

"Do you have another question?" Grace asked. "Inquire about wrongly disgracing a celebrity and profiting from it."

I looked at Richard and wondered aloud, "How about it? Did you enjoy it?"

Richard glared at me and hissed, "Of course I did. I got paid, didn't I? I nailed those smug bastards. They all deserved what they got. And you! I know who you are, James Kimble. I have read the reviews of your books. You're pathetic. The *Grime* trilogy—what a load! The worst books ever. You will never be the true wordsmith that I am. You're nothing."

"Do you see how he dispensed verbal pain?" Grace asked. "He is trying to overcome his fear by injuring you. This is weak behavior. Do you feel the evil coming out of his soul?" She handed me the heating element and continued, "This is a Swiss-made soldering iron used by soldiers in World War II to fix telephone wires. It uses kerosene; no electricity is required. Try burning him on the side," she suggested, as though she were asking me to pick a flower.

I was now holding the soldering iron, but there was no emotional connection. I looked back at Richard in his cage. "I knew it," he said. "You don't have the guts! Barbara, honey, will you please reconsider my offer to help you? I know we can turn this whole thing around." He gave a big grin and continued, "Together, we can do this."

Richard was now nodding and doing his best to smile at Grace. I reached out and touched the soldering iron to his side. Richard seemed surprised, and he screamed in pain. Causing pain felt good, so I burned him with more force in the belly, making him scream even more.

I looked at Grace; she was studying me with great interest. I was now enjoying the experience, so I did it again, and Richard screamed louder. He stammered, "H-hey, stop it! C-come on!"

Grace put her hand on my arm to stop me and took the soldering iron. I gave her a big grin and said, "Wow, that was a rush. Is that what this is all about?"

Grace looked disappointed. She then handed me the same hammer she had used on the other man. "Wait!" Richard pleaded. "No, this isn't right. We can settle this. I have money. You can have it all. Really you can. Just take it. It's yours. All yours."

Richard did his best to smile at me. "No," I said. "I do not want your blood money!"

Richard continued, "All right, all right. You got me! Yoooou got me. Maybe I hurt one girl, and maybe my articles about celebrities weren't completely fact-checked. I confess."

Grace looked at me again. I now knew what I needed to do. My mind had focused to a razor-sharp point. I was now entirely intent on killing this evil man. *I had to do this! I would do this!* He was a parasite with no morals, and killing him was the correct action! It was my right to do this!

Richard could see the change in my expression. "So, we good?" he asked with a smile.

I gripped the hammer and swung it toward Richard with all my might. Unfortunately, my blow smashed into the cage instead of his head. My mind had focused, but my body did not work correctly. Richard, panicked, was desperately pleading. "Hey, stop this! Help me out. We're both writers. We can all work on this together and come up with a solution. Please stop. I'm begging you." A moment later, he pleaded, "I will do anything. Any . . . thing."

Richard tried to smile, and I swung again. At the last moment, he unexpectedly jerked, and the hammer caught his jaw. I actually caught myself smiling at my mistake. Richard screamed and tried to say something, but his mouth was a bloody mess, and no intelligible words came out. I took careful aim, and this time I hit him square on the temple. At that last moment, our eyes met. It gave me a deep, chilling connection to the man I knew as Richard.

I looked at Grace. It was hard to read her expression. *What had I done?* I started shaking as thoughts of pleasure and guilt fought each other in my head. Grace unlocked the cage and undid Richard's restraints. The body flopped to the ground. Grace picked Richard up with ease and threw him face up on the table.

The act of killing released some of my crazy mental pressure. I dropped the bloody hammer with a sense of relief. I could now relax and think about what had happened. I still wondered how a woman with a normal build could toss a big guy like a pillow. Strangely, this observation was paramount in my mind instead of the fact that I had hit a man with a hammer and felt justified in doing so. *Was justified the correct word? Honor bound? Or was it pure fun?* I did not know the answer.

Grace handed me a scalpel, and I noticed an intensity about her. She pointed above the middle of his chest and said, "Make a cut here."

I was unsure, as the cut she had made before was in the back. "When you gain more skill," she explained, "you can work from the back of the body. But for now, you must work from the front. There is more room in the body cavity from this angle. Now cut!"

I did not know why, but I made a large incision. I felt an enormous rush of excitement, and my mind had cleared even more. Blood gushed everywhere. Fortunately, Grace had given me her leather apron, mask, and gloves. I did not remember putting them on. Grace stared at me, and I could feel her thoughts: Do you remember the next step?

I made the incision bigger. I could see the lungs and the area near the heart moving. I looked at Grace, and she motioned for me to continue. I reached in and found what looked like a kidney. I pulled at it to make it more visible. Grace moved the lantern for a better view. There was a noise from the man, and I saw movement in his eyes.

Using a scalpel, I cut out the top of the kidney to remove the adrenal gland. I did my best to scoop the blood away and move the organs around. Once the adrenal gland was cut out, the kidney slid back into his chest. I placed the bloody adrenal gland mass into the teacup.

Now a vast amount of blood was pooling everywhere. This made it difficult to see what I was doing. So I gingerly searched and found the pancreas. Then I cut out the pancreas, resulting in even more blood. I put the bloody mass in the teacup. Afterward, I cut out a section of the kidney and placed it in another teacup.

I could tell that my technique did not impress Grace. However, I was not concerned if she cared or not. Sounding annoyed, Grace said, "You know what is next."

I looked at Richard and could not tell if he was conscious, but I could see movement in his heart and lungs. From behind, I tilted his head upward and, using the V-shaped knife, jabbed at the base of his skull. His body began a slow spasm. The man known as Richard was no more.

Strangely, I felt much better. Then, slowly, a thought occurred to me: I had just killed a person. This entire event should have been terrible. However, to me, it was neither good or bad. I did my reprehensible act with the same effort I would have used to change the channel on the television.

Grace looked at me and yelled, "Hurry up! Time is critical."

I went back to the three teacups and started the preparation process. I took the cup with the kidney and almost added the mint liquid. Grace held my hand to stop me and pointed to the excess tissue that I'd cut out along with the kidney. "You do not need this much," she stated. "Cut off that unnecessary material. Preparation is exceedingly critical."

I cut the tissue away from the kidney to make it appear neat, and this seemed to please Grace. When she pointed to the teacup, I added the mint oil. I then stirred the mixture, and the color changed. My state of mind was making it difficult to concentrate, and I felt anxious. I then picked up the teacup with the adrenal gland, cut some of the tissue off, and gently squeezed it with the two sticks. A thought then occurred to me, and I turned to her and asked, "Do I need to cut the pancreas in half?"

Grace smiled, knowing I was paying attention, and she responded, "You noticed I used one pancreas for the two of us. But a full pancreas will work well for one."

I was too focused to care. With the bloody liquid carefully squeezed out, I turned my attention to Alfred, the cobra. I walked over to the cage and was about to stick my hand in without considering the mortal danger. Fortunately, Grace grasped my hand, handed me an aluminum stick with a grabber on the end, and said in a soft voice, "I got this for you."

I ignored the kind gesture and used the grabber to get Alfred by the tail. Grace looked at me with disapproval and admonished, "Try again."

Eventually, I grabbed Alfred near his head. He was twisting, hissing, and obviously upset. I manipulated Alfred closer to the cup, and Grace suggested, "Touch the back of the fang to the side of the cup. Only one drop."

I did not care at that moment and would have let a gallon flow. Fortunately, only a drop went in. I put the hissy Alfred back in his box. I carefully stirred the liquid, and it congealed like it had done before.

I took the pancreas and carefully trimmed away the unnec-essary tissue. Next, Grace showed me how to remove some additional blood vessels. Then, I added the minty liquid to the adrenal snake liquid and carefully stirred it together. The por-tions of each liquid seemed all right to my untrained eye, but I did not care about perfection—or much else.

Grace motioned toward the doctor's chair. She placed the teacups next to the chair on a small table. I took off my leather apron, which was now completely covered in blood, and then peeled off my jacket, shirt, gloves, and face mask. Grace looked at the incision, removed the bandage, and motioned for me to continue

When Grace turned on the light, I adjusted the mirrors, and I could clearly see my incision. I looked carefully and noticed a fair amount of healing had occurred. To me, this significant amount seemed out of place. There were a pair of small scissors on the table, and I tried to cut the sutures, but everything was backward. In addition, my body was still not working correctly. Grace offered no assistance. I jabbed and snipped and eventually could cut near the knot of the two sutures. There were a pair of tweezers on the table, which I used to remove the sutures. I was in a hurry to get everything finished up, but it still seemed to take forever.

I got a scalpel and made a cut along the previous line. This action was not cold like before. My work was clumsy, causing a lot of pain and a river of blood. Grace still offered no help. Finally, I realized I had not cut correctly and bravely went in for another try. My second cut allowed enough of an opening to see inside.

I used the copper spoon tool to dig around until I had something. Seeing the shriveled-up black mass come out stunned me. I was not sure if it was the same prepared pancreas from the previous "operation" or not.

I used another copper spoon to put the prepared pancreas in and almost dropped it twice, still clumsy with everything backward in the mirror. The incision was now bleeding pro-fusely. A typical person would have been worried about passing out from blood loss, but I did not care. Eventually, I got the pancreas inside my wound and removed the spoon. Next, I took the black stick, dipped it into the liquid, and vigorously applied it inside. Grace directed, "Not too much."

The liquid seemed to make my incision feel better. Grace handed me a curved needle that had thread attached to it. I tried to stitch up my shoulder, but doing this backward was terribly difficult. I was losing a lot of blood, and this did not help. After eleven tedious tries, I looped a single stitch through the opening and tie it off. I used a pair of scissors to snip off the thread.

Grace handed me another curved needle with thread. It took only five tries to make the second stitch. I tied a second knot, snipped off the excess, and made four more sutures. Some blood was still coming out, but the incision was closed. I fin-ished with a sizeable amount of antiseptic and a big bandage. The entire process left me mentally and physically exhausted.

I looked up and realized it would be sunrise soon. I did not know how long we had been there or even what day it was. I tried to get up, but a firm hand from Grace kept me down. "Rest a minute," she said soothingly.

Grace cleaned up and put everything back in its place. She then held my arm to steady me as I got up. The world was spinning, but I was feeling a little better. As we started walking, I looked at the man I knew as Richard and asked, "What about him?"

Grace smiled and replied, "I'll take care of him later."

We went back to the house and sat outside. She had placed a towel over the chair to protect the fabric from my bloody clothing. Grace then brought out a different drink and a small plate with cheese and small pieces of bread. Grace described the origin of the cheese and the type of tea, but I could not focus. I do not remember changing clothes, taking a bath, or the pain of my incision, but I remember when my head hit the pillow. It was such a relief that this ordeal was over. I fell asleep immediately.

SIX

When I awoke, the room was no longer spinning. I felt good. Really good! It was my best night's sleep ever. I let my eyes adjust to the light, sat up, and things seemed all right—actually, better than all right. The incision in my shoulder still hurt, but my normal morning aches and pains were not present.

I got up and noticed a pillow in the corner of the room. As my eyes adjusted, I saw several bird patterns sewn into the fabric. It hit me that one of them was the hummingbird Grace had been working on. My ex-wife sewed, and I knew how projects like that required. I figured sewing the pillow by hand must have taken about a week and a half, working eight hours per day. *Had I really been in this house for that long? How did I figure out "a week and a half" so quickly?*

My first question for Grace was going to be what day it was. I got out of bed, and something else had changed: My football knee injury was not acting up. Well, it was not actually a "football injury." In high school, I had been taunting our football team from the sidelines, an idiotic move on my part. One linebacker took offense, and on the next play, he "accidentally" ran into me. The school treated it as an "accident," but the injury took several months to heal.

There was another neat pile of clothes, this time wrapped in a blue cloth. It was a crazy mix of blue pants, a black shirt, and a gray undershirt. The effect was a distinguished phone-company-repair-gentleman meets old-time-Russian-soldier look, but I was getting used to Grace's clothing style.

I looked in the mirror, and I had changed. My face was tauter, and the look was more defined. I may have been crazy, but I really looked younger. Even my hair looked great, and it was always a mess in the morning. I went into the bathroom to shave, wash up, and use the toilet. To my surprise, my urine was cloudy-white and smelled horrible. I flushed twice and did not know what to think about the smell.

I went to the kitchen. It was empty, but I smelled fantastic bread cooking. The daylight coming in the kitchen windows told me it was midday. I walked past the dining room and found Grace on the sofa, reading. She did not look up as I entered.

Grace looked somehow different. The lines around her eyes had faded, and her nose and ears no longer had the "lost a boxing match" appearance. I stared at her for a moment and sat down. She seemed to be content reading.

I realized the paintings and other art had changed. I noticed one that looked like an original Andy Warhol and got up to get a better look. I know little much about art, but this had to be his best. The date on the painting was April '62. Grace said, "Can you believe Andy only wanted $8 thousand? I talked him down to $5 thousand. It is a prime example of his talent."

I turned around, and I was face to face with her. I do not know how she got from the sofa to inches behind me without making a sound. *Was I ever going to figure out her ability to move?*

Grace gave a thin smile, returned to where she had been sitting, and picked up her book. While thinking about the book she wanted me to write, I asked, "Would now be a good time to begin the interview process?"

Grace did not look up from her book. "I could get my notebook and laptop and start taking some notes," I suggested. Again, no response, so I persevered, "We could start with why you put this thing in my shoulder and why you chose me."

Grace remained silent. I sat down and picked up a book lying nearby. It was in Chinese, or at least a language that looked like Chinese. I thumbed through it; there were some interesting pictures of what appeared to be battle scenes. Grace seemed content with her reading.

I got the impression that Grace was waiting for me to do something. Then I realized this was a *Karate Kid* kind of moment, where I should come to a realization after substantial effort. So I sat quietly for a while and contemplated everything that had happened, but I came up with no answers.

At one point, I got the feeling I was being watched. I looked around and, for a brief instant, I thought I saw a shadow near the door. I stared hard, looking for more movement, but convinced myself it was a crazy feeling.

I was frustrated from not doing anything, but I did not want to upset Grace, so I was tactful. "Would you like something to drink?" I asked and did not get a response. "I could make some tea," I offered. Again, no response.

"Well, it was a long night for me, and I am a bit thirsty," I added. "May I see if there is something in the refrigerator?"

Grace ignored my request and put me back on track: "We will start from the beginning."

I was happy to get a response from Grace. Then, trying to assert some authority as a writer, I asked, "Well, could we discuss your parents?"

Grace put the book down, scowling. She squinted her eyes and answered in a low tone, "You asked me why I chose you for this task. This means that you do not know the answer. We will begin with *your* parents."

Grace picked up her book and continued to read. She always seemed to know exactly how to keep me off guard. Grace had probably been a boxer or master chess player in a former life. She was still reading, and I did not even know what book was in her hands.

I collected my thoughts and asked, "You want to know about my life?" Grace did not look up. "Well, there is not much to tell," I continued, "My parents both worked for the government, and we moved around a lot. My mother, Kim, met my father, Dudley, at an inventory assessment trade convention. I was born in Chicago."

Grace was still not looking up, and I continued in my most cheerful voice, "I suppose you are interested in how I grew up. Well, my childhood was typical for a kid who moved around a lot. I got into many fights because I was the new kid.

"When we were in Arizona, my father made me take a karate class because I kept complaining about the school bully. Eventually, I stood up to him and, with one well-placed punch, knocked him out cold. I got a one-week suspension for starting a fight. The worst part was that the fight started when his two friends held me down, and the bully kicked me. Anyway, after that knockout, nobody bothered me for a few months. Then I switched schools, and it started all over again."

Grace's lack of response annoyed me, but I continued in my most confident voice, "I have a sister and brother. We stuck together as children, but my brother drifted out of our lives. Growing up was difficult for us because we moved all the time. My sister loved to play jokes on me. Some of them were really mean."

Grace did not look up from her book, but I could tell that she nodded and said, "Older sisters often do that."

I was annoyed and informed Grace, "My sister is four years younger than me."

While I could not see Grace's face, I could tell she was smiling. Her hint of pleasure kept me going. "I had an interest in writing and got a partial scholarship to UCLA. My college experience was typical—lots of drinking, parties, great friends, and figuring out what the professors wanted. I majored in journalism with minors in English and literature. After college, I found it difficult to get a job. There were over thirty people in my graduating class alone who majored in journalism, so I had to move back in with my parents in Portland. I was lucky to get a job at the *Portland Tribune.* But that only lasted two weeks because my material did not impress my boss. Looking back on it, I probably oversold myself in the interview."

Grace continued reading, occasionally turning a page. Her indifference was upsetting, but I took a deep breath and forged on, "I needed to move out of my parent's house, so I begged a friend to help get me a job at Best Buy. I started at the bottom and moved up to home-theater sales. In the meantime, I started a computer blog and wrote articles for magazines and the local community paper. I wrote three short books that were rejected by publishers, so I self-published them online. I must admit my first books weren't that great, and they only made a few hundred dollars."

I could tell that Grace was smiling again. That must be her game: cover the smile with a book. I was getting more annoyed, but I was on a roll. "Most of my books and stories were all fantasy. I especially enjoyed writing about trolls, as they're mischievous. Anyway, I got some traction on my blogs, mainly when I talked about popular political events. People seemed to like my casual attitude toward big world changes.

"With the money I made working at Best Buy, I moved into an apartment. Eventually, one of my coworkers sold me his small house. He was going through a complex divorce and sold me the house for less than it was worth. The deal was that I would purchase the house and give him a grand a month in cash for six years. This apparently made his divorce go more smoothly."

Grace's eyes briefly moved over the top of the book, and then she returned to reading. Finally, I must have said something that interested her. I forced a smile and continued, "One night, I was at a party hosted by somebody who liked my blog. During the evening, I met an amazing girl named Heather Harrington. She was cute and had a great sense of humor. We were both twenty-six, and we immediately hit it off.

"She had graduated with a degree in fashion from the Parsons School of Design in New York. That is supposed to be the best and most expensive fashion school in the United States. Heather's father got her a scholarship through his employer.

"Like me, Heather couldn't find a job related to her major and ended up working in the Sears clothing department. Also, like me, she was trying to better herself by selling quilts and custom dresses."

Grace was showing less interest which disappointed me, but I tried to be pleasant. "She moved in with me," I continued, "A year later, we got married, and things were going well. Our life wasn't that exciting. I would write, and she would quilt. We would eat and watch TV. Not much else.

"One day, I wrote a book that actually sold. Suddenly, our lives went through a massive change. Heather couldn't deal with my success, and our relationship went downhill. We ended our three-year marriage, and Heather moved back in with her parents.

"The divorce was messy, and while that was going on, I wrote two more books. I continued to work at Best Buy because my books did not make enough to live on. Plus, my divorce was costing a fortune. My financial situation was so bad I had to take in two roommates. The good news is that the day I met you, my divorce finalized, and soon I can start saving money."

Grace closed her book with a dramatic bang and looked up at me. I knew she was upset—really upset, and I felt a chill run up my spine. Eventually, she chided, "You have told me nothing. Instead, you repeated your lofty book biography and the rest I read on your annoying blog. Tell me more about the person inside you. Tell me why you are here. Tell me why you are not a talented writer."

"But . . . that's the story of my life," I stammered. Grace was clearly frustrated. She picked up her book and said without looking up, "Tell me how you could have prevented your divorce. And this time, speak the truth!"

This was not the direction I wanted the conversation to take. I hoped to change the subject and start the interview process. However, I thought for a moment and took a more honest approach. "In retrospect, our separation started a year before my first successful book. Heather was in charge of our finances. We agreed that a percentage of our Sears and Best Buy incomes would go toward her sewing and my writing. The rest of our money went into savings for a new house.

"I was making $50 to $300 per month on my blogs, articles, and books. However, despite working hard, Heather was not making much money from her sewing projects. She sold a few quilts, but that was mainly to friends. Her dresses did not sell, even to her friends. Heather tried to get small retail outlets interested and was harshly rejected. This failure depressed her, and she was often angry."

Grace seemed less interested, and I continued, "The big blowup happened when I got my first royalty check for *Grime: The Big Hate*. It was for $800, and I was excited beyond belief. I even jumped up and down. We celebrated that night by going out to dinner.

"The next day was a Saturday, and Heather left early in the morning. When she came back in the late evening, she had bags of clothes, a new haircut, and a new purse. She proudly announced that she had thrown away her old purse and bought a 'Prada bag.' I didn't know what a 'Prada bag' was or how much they cost. Heather said we were now living on easy street and the credit card company was happy to advance her any amount. Her attitude shocked me, and I asked her how much she had spent that day. She answered $3,500 like it wasn't an issue.

"Up to that point in our marriage, Heather had held me to a strict budget. Every week, we had a finance meeting to discuss what we had spent, to the penny. For example, I wanted a new refrigerator, as our old one leaked and the ice maker didn't work. I had found a damaged Best Buy store return on clearance for $150 with my employee discount. But Heather insisted that the old one was *fine*.

"I brought this up, and Heather said that now we could afford twenty new refrigerators. I got really upset, and we got into a huge argument. We both were low-key people, and this was our first major blowup. Finally, I drew the line and told her she would have to return all the purchases.

"Heather got furious and declared that our marriage wasn't working. Then she told me she had been sleeping with my friend Jake. He was the guy who helped get me the job at Best Buy, and he had always been there for me. Why Jake, of all people?

"Frustrated and angry, I told her that Jake had AIDS. Of course, this wasn't true; it was an inside joke. But it scared Heather to death, and then she got furious when she realized it was a joke. So she took her new purse and stormed out of the house.

"That night, I went into action. I called all my Best Buy friends, and together we formed a plan. First, we borrowed the work delivery truck and photographed and packed up all of Heather's belonging. I couldn't believe how much quilting stuff she had. It was all new and carefully hidden in boxes. We then brought all our financial paperwork to the Best Buy copy center and made organized duplicates.

"I called Heather's brother and found out that she was staying at her parents' house. So we brought all of her possessions to her parents' house at 9:30 that Sunday morning. We took photographs of everything as we dropped it all on their driveway."

Grace had returned to her book. "One of the little Best Buy scams I'd invented was to damage a new TV or another appliance. I cut one wire and glued it back together. An unsuspecting customer would then return the "broken" appliance because it didn't work. Then, one of us would purchase the appliance at a massive discount. That Monday, we set up Jake to get caught doing this scam. My Best Buy friends aren't the greatest people in the world, but we're tight and don't sleep with each other's wives."

Grace was now intently interested in her book. I took a moment to contemplate and continued, "My manager congratulated us all on getting rid of a *problem* employee. He also recommended a divorce attorney.

"I called Heather's manager at Sears to say that we were separating. She seemed shocked and disappointed. I told her we had a considerable amount of new fabric with a Sears label and no receipts for the merchandise. I knew she couldn't have purchased all of this with our meager income and keep an eye on Heather. Her manager thanked me profusely.

"I then went to the bank and closed the joint account. It had about 50 bucks, and I thought Heather had gotten there first. However, the bank manager told me the account always had the minimum balance.

"I went to the brokerage account to close out our mutual funds and discovered the account never existed. There should have been 75 grand for a new house."

Grace appeared intent on her book. Though annoyed by her lack of interest, I did my best to remain pleasant. "While putting together all the paperwork for the separation, I discovered that our tax statement showed a $120 thousand loss for the prior year. Included were receipts for five sewing machines, expensive fabric, and pricy clothes. In addition, I found a single $80 quilt sale for that year. I had copies of notes from our weekly meetings that showed Heather had sold twenty-one quilts for $200 each. Her deception blew me away.

"My divorce attorney seemed happy with all the paperwork and photographs I put together. He set a date, and we went to court. To our surprise, Heather had hired a pricy attorney. I did not understand how she could afford anything, as she spent all our money. I had to take out a second mortgage and borrow from friends and family to pay for my legal matters.

"Unfortunately, the judge they assigned to us had the reputation of always siding with the wife. The case started out normally by recording lots of documents. My attorney warned me in advance to be super respectful to the judge and let him do all the talking unless asked a direct question.

"We met the judge in her office. Immediately, I could tell that she did not like me, hated authors, and hated my attorney."

Grace looked over the top of her book for a moment. I took this to be a good sign and continued, "Heather's attorney then dropped a bombshell by asking for a $10 million payment from me. At first, the judge seemed willing to grant this outlandish request, which left me in shock. Every time the word 'million' was uttered, my attorney firmly grasped my arm to keep me quiet.

"It was the most frustrating thing ever, but my performance seemed to amuse the judge. I felt like screaming, 'I work at Best Buy! Where the heck am I going to get $10 million?' At one point, the judge asked Heather's attorney about the $120 thousand loss. I wanted to bring up my forged signature, but my attorney didn't let me. Instead, we produced copies of all the receipts. Then, my attorney discreetly pointed to the tax return signature and my signature on another document. When the judge slightly raised her eyebrow, my smile must have broken a world record.

"Heather's attorney became shocked and spoke with Heather in private. This side discussion clearly annoyed the judge. I thought this was a good omen. The judge then asked about the money I got from book sales, and we produced the documents. We also produced an estimated earnings statement from my publisher stating that the book was expected to have sales of ten grand over the next year.

"Heather's attorney flipped out, and again they talked in private. At that point, the judge was visibly upset and started tapping her pencil like a schoolteacher trying to get the class to pay attention. Heather's attorney wanted to contest the statement from my publisher. My attorney said Bethany's phone number was included in the letter, and they were welcome to call her. Heather's attorney assured me that she would contact her that afternoon."

Grace perked up and started listening intently. "We then discussed quilt sales, and my attorney produced the tax forms claiming eighty dollars in sales. We then produced emails, letters, and other documents showing twenty-one quilts were sold for $200 each. Finally, as proof, I suggested the judge call all of Heather's friends and ask if they had purchased quilts.

"Heather got really upset and started arguing with the judge. Then, to my horror, Heather swore at the judge. I wanted to intervene, but my attorney firmly dug his fingernails into my arm to keep me silent.

"The judge calmly pressed a button on her desk. A bailiff appeared and dragged Heather out while she was still swearing. Without skipping a beat, the judge continued with the proceedings. Later, the judge asked us for a copy of my pay stubs. I forgot to bring them and apologized profusely. I then told her I would work all night if necessary to make sure she had copies in the morning. The judge seemed modestly impressed by this assurance."

Grace had returned to reading her book. I could not figure out the pattern of what Grace found interesting and what she did not. I kept talking. "What it basically came down to was that neither of us had any assets. Heather had spent our entire savings on her failed quilting effort.

"The only other asset was the house. It had a second mortgage, and the house itself wasn't worth much. In the end, the judge decided I should keep the house, along with both mortgages. Heather would keep the sewing machines and fabric. In addition, I would pay Heather ten grand over three years. I thought this was completely unfair, but my attorney was ecstatic. Heather immediately contested the decision. In Oregon, it's a complex and expensive process to challenge a divorce settlement. At that point, I was sure my divorce was over and that I could move on.

"My life returned to normal. I was still working at Best Buy and had completed writing my second book. Unfortunately, Heather hadn't fared so well. Jake was never really into her, and she lost her job at Sears. Apparently, she had missed a lot of work, and her boss suspected her of stealing.

"Eventually, the contested decision came before a different judge. The argument was that my book was secretly selling for millions of dollars. There was no evidence presented, and the judge threw out the case. Heather cussed out this new judge, and he threw out the ten grand I owed her. That really made me happy, as I had no way to pay her. I had borrowed money from everybody to pay my attorney. I was working extra shifts and even selling peppermint crackers on eBay. Who knew you could sell crackers on eBay?

"After that, we went our separate ways. I found out through a mutual friend that Heather's best friend got her a teller job at a local bank. My second book was in bookstores and was actually selling well. This extra income allowed me to start paying back everybody I owed money to."

Grace was reading, which annoyed me, but I kept telling my story. "Things had finally returned to normal. Then, out of the blue, Heather filed a $100 million civil case, naming me, Jake, Best Buy, Sears, my attorney, the first judge, the second judge, her divorce attorney, her contested-decision attorney, my publisher, and my father as defendants. The lawsuit was a complete mess and made the local paper.

"I had absolutely no money and had tapped out my friends. My attorney, 'against his better judgment,' agreed to take on the case and said he would loan me the money for his services. This of course, came at a modest interest rate under a signed, notarized payment contract. He said he had never done this before, but he appreciated my prompt payment in the past. I also got the feeling he didn't like being sued.

"In under a week, the judge removed the corporations, attorneys, and judges from the lawsuit. That left me, my father, and Jake. Jake promptly left town without telling anybody (including his family) where he went. My father threatened a countersuit naming Heather's attorney, and the judge removed him from the lawsuit. To this day, he remains angry with me for somehow dragging him into this. I have no idea why Heather included him in the lawsuit. Up to that point, my father got along well with Heather.

"We asked for an evidentiary hearing to see what the legal argument was. Heather's attorneys produced a staggering amount of well-researched publishing industry financial documents. All my book sales were subpoenaed and presented. Heather had two attorneys and expert witnesses in economics, publishing, and asset hiding. We asked to see exactly how they justified a $100 million lawsuit. The judge said he would get back to us."

Grace seemed bored, sipped some tea, then went back to her book. I was getting hungry, but I decided not to discuss the matter. "My attorney said that this case—with three expert witnesses and two attorneys—must cost Heather over a $100 grand. I went to the bank where Heather worked and spoke with the manager. I told him that Heather was living way beyond her means, and she had to be getting the money somewhere. The manager didn't believe me and demanded I leave the premises.

"I then arranged a meeting with Heather's father. Before the breakup, we had been tight. We both liked to talk about horror movies and cars. He agreed to have coffee at a local diner. When we met, he looked upset and said that I 'had quite a lot of nerve' asking to see him. When I asked why he was so upset, he said that I was hoarding hundreds of millions of dollars.

"This accusation was so upsetting that I had to get up and pace. I sat back down and told him I would give him copies of every check I'd received over the last ten years, including the small ones from publishers and my blog. I told him that the total amount from all my publishing efforts to date was under $30 grand.

"My admission stunned him. He spilled his coffee and had trouble breathing. He looked confused and said that Heather told him I was making almost a million dollars every month and that she had solid evidence. I laughed really loud and said that Heather lived in a fantasy world and I would never make a million bucks, no matter what I did.

"I told him that as proof, he could come by my house: I removed half of my light bulbs to save money. I also told him that I was so desperate to pay the heating bill I sold my spare tire for ten dollars on Craigslist. I dared him to go out to my beat-up old car and check for a spare.

"He became despondent and told me that to pay for the three attorneys, he had liquidated their retirement savings, maxed out his credit cards, and borrowed all the money he could against his house. Heather had promised to pay it all back with buckets of money to spare. He said he was utterly ruined and cried.

"I had a deep respect for this man, and seeing him cry made me feel small. Then, he thanked me for the coffee and left.

"Three days later, my attorney told me that the judge saw no reason to continue the case. Two weeks later, Heather and her friend lost their jobs; apparently, they both stole from the bank."

After my personal outpouring, Grace closed her book. Then, with an icy stare, she said, "Tell me about your book." I asked if I could have a bite to eat. Grace gave me a disappointed look and pointed toward the kitchen.

I went to the kitchen, opened the refrigerator, and noticed that a light came on. *Where was the electricity coming from? Why was the house lit with oil lamps?*

Inside I saw lots of neatly arranged food. I found it interesting that only one item was in a store container. There was a side of farm-cured ham, and I used a knife to cut a small portion off. I found several loaves of homemade bread and made myself a sandwich. Finally, I poured something purple from a pitcher into a glass that I found in a cabinet.

There was no table or chair I could use to sit and eat in the kitchen, so I ate over the sink. It tasted amazing—the bread was so fresh, and the drink tasted like berry heaven. Grace sneaked up behind me, and she startled me by saying, "You are drinking out of a measuring cup and getting crumbs everywhere."

I apologized, and she said in an angry voice, "Finish your food, clean up your mess, and we will continue."

I cleaned the three bread crumbs off the floor. Yes, I actually counted the number of bread crumbs. I then sat back down and talked about my book. "The *Grime* series was set . . ."

Grace held up her hand. I could tell she was agitated, and she cautioned me, "Keep in mind that I have read your books. You went from writing about useless trolls set in a silly, made-up world to a well-researched story set in eighteenth-century England. Reveal your true motivations."

I thought for a moment and cheerfully said, "Well, it seemed like an important time in history."

Grace again held up her hand. This time I could tell I had crossed a line. "You know I understand when you are lying," she admonished. "Tell me the truth. Right now!"

I paused for a long time. This was a painful subject, and I did not want to tell her—or anybody—the truth. Then, I looked into her eyes, and I knew what she would say next: *I could get out the soldering iron, and you will talk.* I must have given her a look of horror because her expression changed from anger to irritation.

I paused, took a deep breath, and began in a low voice, "My writing efforts hadn't been successful. I was kicking around new ideas and trying new subjects on my blog. Nothing was working. I even considered giving up writing and taking some economics courses at the local community college. One day . . ." I looked away from Grace and then continued in a barely audible voice, "I was walking around our neighborhood, and there was a garage sale. It was actually an estate sale. The father had died, and his children were selling off his stuff.

"One thing for sale was a box of typed paper. The pages looked really interesting, and I hoped to get some story ideas. I bought the entire box for five bucks. The family was happy to get the money, as nothing else was selling. I dreaded bringing the box home; I knew that spending a small amount of money without permission would upset Heather. She wanted everything accounted for; we even packed our own lunches to save money."

Grace seemed upset that I had gone off on a tangent. I desperately did not want to continue. Finally, I looked away and whispered, "Inside the box were several short stories, one completed book, part of a sequel, and lots of notes. I took the completed book, changed some of it, and made up a new title: *Grime: The Big Hate*. All my brilliance came from that stupid box."

I felt ashamed, but a tremendous weight was lifted. I had never revealed that I had taken the credit for another writer's work. Of course, a true writer never steals, but I was desperate. Or at least that was what I told myself. I wanted to be a successful writer so bad that I took advantage of the situation.

I looked at Grace; she wore a strange, wicked smile. *Was she happy that she had broken me?* I looked down and said slowly, "I checked with the Library of Congress, and Jack Waldron Dunkin was a hack writer in the '50s and '60s. He had a few short stories in magazines but no books. He originally entitled his work, *An Oxford Tale of Mischief*. Several critics pointed out the areas I had changed as the worst parts of the book. I had hoped that a title with the word 'grime' would invoke edginess, but my publisher Bethany disagreed. I persisted, and she printed the book with the 'Grime' title. The critics also criticized the title as weak.

"I took his partially completed sequel and finished it. I called it *Grime: Just Cause.* This book sold better than the first book. However, the critics disliked the parts of the book that I wrote. I still remember one particularly mean blogger called the ending, 'the work of a stuttering child.' I wrote the third book, *Grime: At the End.* It has received dreadful reviews. Most of my fans feel it's a poor rewrite of the first book."

Grace was smiling. I took this as a bad sign. I had expected her to talk about the magnitude of my failure and how I was a rotten person. I was also expecting her to say I was not good enough to write her story. Instead, she looked at me for a long time before speaking. "Look at all the pain you caused. You plagiarized your book, your wife no longer loves you, you are in debt, you caused your wife to lose two jobs, her friend lost her job, you lost your friend Jake, Jake left town, you stole from Best Buy, your father-in-law is in prodigious debt, your father dislikes your choices, and the family of a great writer never knew how great he actually was. Your only reward was a pittance and minor celebrity status."

That statement hit me like a baseball bat. It was far more upsetting than my shoulder being cut open. Tears flowed, and I put my hands over my face. In the past, I had forced myself not to think in terms of responsibility, but suddenly I realized that my life was a major failure. "How do you respond to this?" Grace asked in an icy voice.

I took a long time to recover before replying. "What you have said is true. I'm a failure, and I have made a mess of things."

"Do you know why I chose you?!" Grace demanded.

No. I did not. I was still absorbing the realization that my outstanding success was actually a massive failure.

Grace let my failure sink in and spoke in an ice-filled voice, "You offer very little and cause great pain to those around you."

I stared at the only blank wall in the room and slowly asked, "But do I deserve to die? Are you going to harvest me?"

Grace smiled and answered, "No, you are not *that* bad. For the first time in your life, you understand what you are and what you are not. This will help you write about who I am. You needed a push to get going in the right direction. We may begin."

SEVEN

Grace looked directly at me and said, "I will bring you your computer and writing materials."

The experience of baring my heart and soul had wiped me out. The last thing I wanted to do was write, so I asked, "Can we sit for a while?"

Grace looked at me for a moment and got up. Outside, it appeared to be late afternoon, and there was a slight breeze. The apple trees looked like they were slowly dancing in the wind. I sat in the chair, staring at nothing in particular.

Grace brought out a noticeably different silver tray and pitcher. She sat with one leg folded on the chair, and we both took a sip. Since Grace had kidnapped me—I did not know how many days ago—I had sampled the best things to eat, so it did not shock me when the drink tasted fantastic. It had a mild lavender scent with a sweet oatmeal base. The drink complimented my depressed mood perfectly.

I looked at Grace and asked, "What day is it?"

"Wednesday at about 4:30," she cheerfully responded. "We will have dinner soon."

I let this sink in and calculated all the days I had slept, trying to make a mental timeline. I could not process it all; there were so many time gaps and so much missing information. I looked at the apple trees and asked without turning to her, "How did you finish the hummingbird pillow so quickly?"

Grace laughed and answered, "That took three months to make. It is part of a set I am working on. Did you think I completed that entire project in the time you have been here?"

I could feel Grace looking at me, and when I turned to her, she had a huge grin. She laughed, and then I laughed. It got so bad that I started making a honking sound. Grace said between laughs, "Wow, you are really out of it."

After some time, the laughs died down, and I said, "I think I get it."

Grace looked amused and asked, "Get what?"

"About the propane tank. You have a generator or something for the refrigerator." Grace laughed again and said, "That is your big revelation? Of course, I do. It is behind the barn in a soundproof shed. You can see the exhaust pipe right there."

She pointed to a thin black pipe. *Why didn't I figure this out before?*

"I also use electricity for the television and computer. Oh, I also have a hairdryer in the master bathroom."

For some reason, the possession of an electric hairdryer was a big revelation. Grace wore an amused expression. She had brought both of her legs up on the chair and wrapped her arms around them. Her head was now resting on her knees, and she had a joyful expression. For the first time, I saw her as a normal woman. She was not the mass-murdering, five-hundred-year-old, torturing, eye-arrow-shooting psychopath. Instead, I saw her as a cute, twenty-something-year-old with a great laugh. *How could this be the same person?*

I realized that if we were at a party, I would have no fear of walking over to Grace and striking up a conversation. So I playfully asked, "You have a computer?"

"Of course," Grace answered with a big grin. "How do you think I found out about you?"

Grace seemed amused by my ignorance. "So, besides reading, gardening, music, cooking, collecting art, and tormenting authors with pillow jokes, what else do you do?" I wanted to know.

Grace laughed and freely answered, "Tormenting authors with pillow jokes? So, you are an author now? I would not go that far. Well, let me see . . . I like to paint, travel, write poetry, manage my investments, manage my properties, gather information on the computer, watch a few television shows and, sometimes, movies. And by the way, you can operate a refrigerator on propane. There is a wonderful book, loosely based on the inventor, called *The Mosquito Coast*."

"I haven't read that book. I'll have to look it up," I said. "May I see one of your paintings?"

Grace smiled and got out of her chair. We walked into a contemporary-looking room with a large skylight. I saw painting materials and a partially completed landscape on an easel. There were several paintings on the wall, all signed by different people. The composition looked different, but the paintings looked to be in the same painting style.

The second one on the left was a dim landscape with bare trees with leaves at their bases. As I was looking, Grace commented, "I painted that example in 1810. I was at an art school near Paris, and this was my third assignment. Not my best work."

"It looks sad," I reflected.

Grace answered in a distant, quiet voice, "Yes, I painted it around the time that a dear friend had died. I brought this painting out of storage recently to mark her passing."

I was looking at the next one. It was an octopus, with each tentacle holding a cryptic symbol. Cyrillic letters surrounded each symbol.

"I am going to answer my own question," I said with a smile. "Is this house a 'get back to nature' place, and that is why there are no electric lights?"

Grace was looking at another painting and commented, "When I paint hair, it does not look good. I need to apply more effort." She turned to me and answered, "I never felt comfortable with electric light. It casts harsh shadows and does not look natural. I grew up with oil light, and to me, a home is not a home without it. Let's cook dinner."

Apparently, the interview was over. Grace took me to a greenhouse, where we picked dark green oregano, bright green basil, and other fresh herbs. Next, we moved outside to pick vegetables and potatoes from the garden. We then made our way into the kitchen. Grace put on an apron with red-cherry embroidery and handed me another one with wheat-grain embroidery.

Grace started humming a gentle tune and opened the refrigerator. She began pulling out food and bottles of liquid and placing them on the counter. Then, Grace started a pot of water boiling and began cutting the vegetables. She looked up and said, "I will make you a dish that my mother used to make. It is called turnip soup with chicken and boiled potatoes. The dish is not fancy, but you will enjoy the flavor."

Grace took out a full chicken and deboned it. She pointed to the tomatoes and made a chopping motion with her hand. I started chopping while Grace was softly humming and preparing the chicken. She showed me how to wrap the chicken in cooking parchment paper, put in the spices and fresh herbs, and placed it in a ceramic pot.

The chopped vegetables went into a frying pan with grape seed oil, and then Grace placed them into a pot. Next, she took heavy cream from the refrigerator and added it. It surprised me to see the cream came out of a mason jar.

After pondering my cooking lesson, I felt enough at ease to ask, "I have a question, but I don't want to upset you." She nodded, and I continued, "I am holding a knife, and you turned away from me. Why are you so comfortable?"

Grace had taken out some dough and was kneading it with her hands as she hummed. Then she looked at me, smiled, and said, "I'm not that defenseless."

Grace's smile grew bigger, and within half a second, I was looking down the barrel of a handgun. It was so close that I could see the grooves in the barrel. Yet, I did not know where the gun came from.

Grace continued to smile and said confidently, "'I'll make you famous.' Do you remember that movie?"

I knew the gun was real, and it was really pointing at me. Graced had asked me a question; what was it? The question was about a movie. *What movie did she ask about?* I vaguely recalled that the quote was from some '80s western.

Grace put the gun in her apron pocket, looked at me with an amused expression, and commented, "There is another quote from the television show *Burn Notice*: 'Guns make you stupid.' The same applies to knives. The incorrect notion is that if you have a weapon, you are in a superior position. In this confident state, people make mistakes. The reason I am so at ease is I know you are not a killer . . . yet."

Grace paused, then added, "When somebody is about to take a life, they become determined. If you know what to look for, this intent is easy to recognize. So you must keep this in mind from now on."

This thought terrified me. Grace resumed humming and then placed the bread on a well-used tray. The potatoes had been boiling for a while, and she strained them. "Do you know what kind of gun that was?" Grace asked in a whimsical voice.

I have played video games and watched many movies, but I never used a gun. I shook my head, and Grace informed me, "It is a Browning Hi Power. That is a nine-millimeter semiautomatic handgun that holds thirteen bullets. A Chinese officer gave that gun to me in the summer of 1948. He became a cook and therefore had no use for it. Since then, I have used that gun to defend myself several times. We will talk about those details later."

We cleaned up the kitchen. The area where Grace had been working took less than a minute to clean, but my "expert" chopping skills scattered vegetable bits everywhere. When the bread came out of the oven, dinner was ready.

In the dining room, Grace set the table, and this answered one of my many questions. It was possible to set the table in less than a minute. Grace mastered rapid organization and coordination. She looked up to see my look of astonishment and asked confidently, "What did you expect? After five hundred years of setting tables, I have perfected the task."

Again, another profound statement that left me with more questions than answers. Dinner, as usual, tasted exceptional. The paper-wrapped chicken was incredibly tender, and the soup, while simple, was the best I had ever tasted. Even the potatoes that I had chopped were exceptional. The fresh bread had a wonderful crunchy crust that seemed to compliment everything. Grace brought out a frozen custard that melted with every bite.

We finished our cleanup, and Grace took out an old brass teakettle. She filled the kettle with water, added tea, milk, honey, and a cut-up green apple, then let it come to a boil. We went into the sitting area, and Grace poured two glasses. She smelled the mixture and was deep in thought for a long moment. Eventually, she said, "That teakettle was my mother's wedding gift, and this drink is called 'shuduka.' That word does not have a modern translation, but you could call it 'sweet tea with apple.'"

We sat down, and I tried to relax. Grace reached behind the sofa and produced my Dawson's Creek notebook and a pen. She smiled and asked, "Shall we begin?"

I was finishing my tea and sheepishly replied, "Sounds good. Where would you like to start?"

After all Grace's avoidance in the past, it surprised me when she began without hesitation. "We will start with my father, Ukrit. A big man with wonderful strong brown hair and dark brown eyes. You would have enjoyed meeting him. He was born twenty-seven years before me, in the summer of 1471, near the small town of Valdai in what we now call Russia. His parents were both potato farmers.

"My father was a private man who did not show emotion. He married young and had a wife before my mother. She died after being kicked by a horse. My father never spoke about her or the incident. I only learned about the details of her passing from a neighbor long after my father passed away. I do not know her name but they had a daughter, and she died young. Many children died from disease, and I suspect that this is how she passed.

"Together, they had my older half-brother, Ujarak. Ujarak means 'like a rock,' and this name suited him well. He was of medium build, with short brown hair and dark green eyes. He loved to hunt and walk in the woods. I have many fond memories of him teaching me how to stalk game and ride horses.

"My family lived on a small farm located near a central road. We had a barn, a well, a horse, two cows, and a forge. My father grew turnips. Some years after my father's first wife passed, there was a loud knocking sound late at night. Lamp oil was expensive, and people were not awake for long periods after sunset. My father opened the door while holding his favorite hammer. Incidentally, this was the same hammer you used two days ago."

I realize this hammer had probably taken the lives of many people. Grace looked at me with amusement and continued, "Outside was a cold and tired woman dressed in fine clothing. She was on her way to visit her cousin when somebody took her horse in a botched robbery. The woman had been walking for hours in the darkness and needed shelter from the cold. She asked my father if she could stay for the night.

"It was not proper for a lady to stay in a stranger's house. Because our small house did not have a spare bed, my father led her to the barn and gave her an old blanket. In the morning, he came out with Ujarak to do the chores. The woman was still asleep and tightly curled in the blanket.

"Later, my brother found her lame horse, and my father had to put it down. The woman, Natalya, was effectively stranded, as my father could not let her use his only horse. Natalya had money to buy a horse, but no horses were for sale. It was harvest time, and without a horse, people would starve during the winter. We later learned that her family had sent out search parties to look for her, but they had searched in the wrong direction, as they thought she visited a different cousin.

"Natalya was an aristocrat from a large family of merchants and did not know how to do chores. However, she was intelligent and learned quickly. Natalya decided to stay with us for half a season until she could purchase a horse. To pay for her board, she did chores, cooked, and worked on the farm.

"Ukrit and Natalya took company, and a year later, I was born, followed by my sister, Nadezhda, and my brother, Timur. My mother was a wonderful woman. She had long, flowing, light-brown hair, beautiful green eyes, and a remarkable figure. Her smile could warm the coldest day.

"Natalya loved the color purple, and while this was not a common color of the day, she always brought this color into our lives. She had an exquisite sense of humor and took great care to see the best in any situation. I enjoyed hearing her laugh.

"My younger sister, Nadezhda, had straw-blond hair and blue eyes, and she was tall for a girl. She loved to ride horses, and we were the closest of friends. My younger brother, Timur, had wiry black hair, and this was his most striking feature. He was tall and skinny and had dark brown eyes like his father. He loved to fish and was the fastest person for miles around. I never beat him in a race, but I tried at every opportunity.

"My mother, being an aristocrat, could read, write, do arithmetic, and she knew history. Every night after dinner, she would educate us. Before my parents met, my father could not read, which was a source of great shame. My mother spent many months teaching him to read. Soon he was the only adult man in our local area who could read proficiently. He would proudly tell this fact to anybody who would listen.

"Eventually, my mother reconnected with her family, and they dropped by from time to time. My family took my mother's family name, Ermolaev, as it brought sophistication to our humble background. Her brother, Octavius, was my favorite. He taught me how to shoot and gave me strips of bear jerky. Because guns and ammunition were expensive, shooting was a rare skill.

"Natalya's older sister did not like my father and only visited once. Natalya's parents visited a few times, but they died when

I was young. People back then rarely lived beyond the age of forty-five. I liked my grandparents because they would give me a small coin every time we met. I still have two and keep them in a safe location.

"Growing up, our favorite pastime was to sit by the road and chat with strangers. We learned about faraway places, news, and gossip. The most popular subject for the travelers was: 'How far is it to Valdai?' I must have answered that question a thousand times over my childhood. I even carved a small sign to inform the travelers. We always gave the same answer: 'a day's ride.'

"Travelers were often hungry, and one day we took some food down the road. It sold quickly, and we sold more the next day. At first, the meals were cut-up turnips from our farm.

"Later, my mother set up an outdoor kitchen next to the road. At the time, there were no restaurants, and people would eat at their homes or at their friends' homes. Even large cities had only a few dedicated restaurants.

"My mother's cooking was an instant success, and people from the surrounding area stopped by. This was the beginning of a business, and soon my father built a restaurant, a wagon repair shop, a sleeping area, a stable, and a blacksmith shop. At the peak of these endeavors, eight people worked for us.

"Soon, my family became moderately wealthy, and we purchased several plots of farmland. Because land ownership was the supreme expression of wealth, my mother's family approved of my father.

"Growing up during this time was wonderful, as I met new people every day, did chores, cooked, cleaned, and learned about many educational subjects from my mother. The part of this story that will interest you will have to wait until morning."

I had gathered a lot of background information, but she had not answered my big questions. I said good night, washed up, and went to bed. I had a lot of thinking to do, but I fell asleep quickly.

In the morning, I woke up, and somebody was in bed with me. Imagining a nice, sexy surprise, I whispered, "Good morning, Grace."

There was no response. I slowly moved the covers and discovered I was sharing my bed with a big, golden-haired dog of a breed I did not recognize. This discovery disappointed me, and I got out of bed.

Again, a package of clothes lay at the foot of my bed. How Grace sneaked in there to bring me clothes, I would never know. As I got dressed, my movements awoke the dog, which was still under the covers. "Come on, pooch, away with you!" I yelled in a silly voice.

Slowly, the dog got out of bed. To my horror, it was not a dog at all. It was a colossal wildcat! I leaped into the corner, terrified of being attacked. The massive animal had huge teeth and gigantic paws with enormous claws. *Was it planning to eat me?*

The big cat stretched, looked at me nonchalantly with its big yellow eyes, and waited for me to open the door. I did so, and the monster casually walked out. I looked down the hall, and it yawned.

I composed myself, shaved, and walked into the kitchen. Grace was feeding the beast raw meat and talking to it in Russian. She had on what I would describe as a white-and-blue sundress. Grace's hair was arranged into a tight bun, and she wore a thin pearl necklace. She said to me, "I would like for you to meet Heathcliff. She is a full-grown mountain lion. We have been together for many years."

"We already met," I replied. "Actually, we slept together."

Grace laughed. "I'm sorry Heathcliff startled you," she said. "She comes and goes as she pleases. This is the first time she has been back in five days. Normally she does not like strangers. She has probably been watching you."

"That's a wild animal . . . you know, the dangerous kind," I muttered.

Amused, Grace replied, "I have been around dangerous animals all my life. I know how to get along with them. A mountain lion is more graceful than a bear or a tiger."

"I thought Heathcliff was a guy's name," I ventured. Grace grinned and nodded.

We made fresh bread and omelets for breakfast. Well, she made the food, and I made a mess. After we finished, I cleaned, and we retired to the room with the sofas. I picked up my Dawson's Creek notebook, and Grace began: "The part of this story that should fascinate you started with a dare. My younger sister and I were walking down the road. Incidentally, the road had a proper name, Energetikov, but we always called it 'the road.' There was a point where the road forked, and this marked a patch of dense forest. The people from the surrounding area said something evil had happened in that part of the forest and was cursed. At that time, folklore ruled over common sense.

"My sister challenged me to walk into this forest until the sun was at its highest and then come back. We often dared each other to perform foolish feats of strength. Most of our challenges involved riding horses and then jumping off. Surprisingly, our dares did not kill us, as there was no such thing as a doctor, and a broken bone was often fatal.

"As a twelve-year-old, I had no fear. I marched right into the forest. It was a wonderful walk, and quite beautiful. Finally, I came to a large clearing near a majestic waterfall flowing into a small lake. I walked over to the lake, intending to look for fish.

"Out of nowhere, a pair of hands grabbed me from behind. I screamed and kicked with all my might, to no avail.

"As I was being dragged, I noticed several of what you would call gypsy carts near several tall trees. A gypsy cart is the six-teenth-century version of a mobile home. These particular carts were of exceptional quality, as the wood was perfectly hand-carved. Many pictures and repeated symbols decorated the outside. The artistic style was strange, and I did not under-stand the significance.

"Even though I met many travelers, I had never run into people who looked like this. Dark-skinned, they wore gold ornaments and white garments that left their arms, legs, and bellies exposed. It was taboo to wear clothing that allowed others to view so much skin.

"One man called out words in a foreign language. I was scared but acted bravely and yelled, 'Let me go!'

The man holding me did not understand my request. Soon, three other men dressed in the same garb came over. The five men brought me over to the largest gypsy cart and forced me to kneel. Then the men kneeled next to me while holding me. I tried to get away, but their grip was firm. They waited quietly while I yelled. Looking back, their patience with their newly captured prisoner was admirable.

"Finally, a person came out of the largest gypsy cart. My captors forced my head down so I could not see who it was. They spoke unfamiliar words and allowed me to rise.

"A young woman of immense beauty stood before me. Her thin face was brown, like theirs, with many striking features. Her long hair was dark black, and she arranged it with jewels and gold. The only parts of her that were not perfect were her nose and ears, as they had some disfigurements. Then I noticed that several of the men shared the nose and ear disfigurements. So I suspected this imperfection was common to their family.

"The woman silently commanded the men which made it clear she was in total control. All the men seemed to fear her, but I remained defiant and continued to struggle. The woman seemed amused at my efforts and motioned toward one of two chairs. The men forced me to sit, and after circling around behind me, the woman gracefully took her seat.

"The woman gazed upon me intently, much as I stared at you at the bookstore. Like you, I was terrified, but I remained defiant and firm. I had resolved that, whatever happened, I would survive and tell my sister I had won the challenge.

"The woman put her hand on her heart and said, 'Cledopart.' She then pointed to me. I put my hand over my heart and said, 'Anitchka.' Since I could not pronounce her name, I pointed to her and said, 'Cleo.' The woman thought for a moment and nodded. Then, she looked amused and said something in a language I did not understand.

"She then said, in basic Russian, 'greetings.' It was clear Cleo did not know more than a few words in my language. So I said, 'greetings' back to her, but I pronounced it correctly.

"She turned and said something to the men. One of them left and brought back a tray. Cleo said something else, and the men released their grip on my shoulder. I thought about running, but when I looked around, I realized escape was impossible.

"The man presented a tray to me, and it had a dark type of food I did not recognize. Cleo took a small bite and motioned for me to try the food. I took a tiny bite, and it had a flavor like nothing I had ever tasted. Later in my life, I realized that this was the first time I had eaten chocolate. Like any ten-year-old girl, I gobbled it up, but I maintained eye contact. My concentration appeared to impress Cleo. We sat for a long while, and she studied me intently.

"At one point, Cleo stood up, motioned for me to follow, and we walked past her large gypsy cart. Further on were sixteen other carts, along with horses. I had never seen so many horses, and they all were the finest in the land. So I concluded Cleo was wealthy.

"We returned to her gypsy cart, and she led me inside. The men appeared to be frightened and averted their eyes when she opened the door. I saw splendid paintings, treasures, and a lavish sleeping area. My father had a single, thin gold coin that he kept in a special place, and it was his most treasured possession. There were small statues made entirely out of gold, paintings in gold frames, and even gold embedded in the floor.

"Cleo seemed amused at my interest. She brought out an enormous book that contained many words in a language I did not understand. However, there were some words in Russian, and we used the book to translate. Our efforts were far from perfect; it took a long time to convey even simple messages. Our interaction went on for several hours.

"Cleo told me she was once a supreme ruler in a far-off eastern kingdom. Her rule was absolute, and she put down anyone who opposed her. Her greatest passion was to become the most beautiful woman in all the land. It was apparent that a deep sense of vanity fueled her. To this end, she performed every type of beauty treatment on her slaves. It was challenging to translate numbers, but Cleo said she performed as many experiments as stars in the sky.

"Some treatments proved successful, and Cleo applied those treatments to herself. The results amazed those around her, and she made an immense effort to ensure others did not learn her beauty secrets.

"Cleo continued to live a happy life ruling over her subjects. However, there was a power struggle in her kingdom. Cleo was not much of a strategist or an organizer, and her oldest son, Caesarion deposed her, which caused great pain. So Cleo faked her death and escaped with a few servants.

"After our conversation, Cleo spoke to the guards. They grabbed me and took me to an area that formed a circle. In the center were a fire, a table, several chairs, and a wooden post. They forced me to sit on one of the chairs.

"About thirty men came to the circle from the surrounding carts. They all had dark skin and were excited to be part of whatever was happening. They wore exotic, colorful clothing and strange shoes that went halfway up their legs.

"An elaborate ceremony started, with dancing and dramatic words. Cleo led the ritual and commanded her subjects by throwing throw small objects into the fire. These objects would suddenly make a 'bang' noise and shower out sparks from the embers. With each eruption, the men jumped and shrieked. Of course, I recognized the smell of gunpowder but did not let on that I understood this trick.

"Cleo performed her dance with closed eyes and precision movements. Her athletic prowess amazed me, as I had never imagined a body could move with such grace. The ceremony both scared and excited the men.

"As the ceremony proceeded, they brought a man with light skin into the circle. His hands were bound, and he wore the clothes of a Russian traveler. They had put red and black markings on his face in an ornate pattern. The man spoke Russian and complained of being mistreated. The men tied him to a log near the fire.

"The dancing continued, and three more light-skinned men with red and black on their faces were brought to the circle. Cleo pointed at me and then said something to the dancing men. They stopped dancing and stared at her in great disbelief.

"Cleo threw more gunpowder into the fire, and they continued to fixate on her. She stood next to me, and suddenly the men gripped me firmly. Cleo pointed to me and spoke one word in Russian: 'special.'

"Suddenly, she thrust a thin knife into my shoulder. The pain was beyond anything I had ever experienced, and I struggled with all my strength. The men continued to hold me down while blood ran down my body. I did not understand what was happening or why. My only thought was I would die soon.

"The men started dancing and singing again. I wanted very much to cry, but I refused to give them the satisfaction. The men seemed to be impressed by my bravery.

"Cleo then took out a large knife and suddenly cut open the first Russian man's chest. Then, to my horror, she started taking living organs out of his chest while he pleaded for his life. She removed the organs and placed them into ornate bronze vessels with black, painted markings. She then did unthinkable things with the bloody organs like the one we performed two days ago.

"With a dramatic move, Cleo threw gunpowder into the fire and thrust her blade into the still-living Russian man's neck. Blood sprayed everywhere, which further excited the dancing men. This was the first time I had ever watched a person die, and I knew my life would end in the same manner.

"A black-colored live snake was then passed from dancing man to dancing man and then finally to Cleo. This sight was unbelievable to me, as it was the first time I had ever observed a person touching a snake. Cleo shocked me by milking the snake into the ornate vessel.

"With a clap of Cleo's hands, all eyes turned to me. The men then forced me into a kneeling position and prevented me from moving. Suddenly, Cleo forced something from the ornate vessel into my shoulder wound. This caused me great pain, and I yelled as loud as I could. Cleo then used a needle and thread to stitch the wound closed.

"This procedure differed slightly from the one that I performed on you because I improved the process.

"Cleo now turned her attention to three Russian prisoners and performed the same procedure. She took the freshly prepared organs and placed them into three of the men in elaborate blue outfits. They appeared to be immensely grateful for this 'gift,' which brought them tears of joy.

"The dancing continued, and I passed out from the pain. When I woke up in total darkness, I thought this blackness was the beginning of heaven.

"I do not know how long I was in the darkness, but a door suddenly opened, and a guard unlocked my chains. I realized I was alive and had been resting in one of their gypsy carts. I got up, and the men now treated me differently, as if I had somehow gained their respect.

"The men served me meat and potatoes. They then allowed me to walk freely among them. At first, it was challenging to move, as my body ached. My shoulder remained in considerable pain, and I did not know what was happening.

"As I walked, I observed all the activity in the immediate area. They prepared food, maintained livestock, and did other chores. Together, they had formed a remarkable community in this remote Russian valley. When I looked closely, I saw each man had a shoulder scar in the same place I was wounded.

"As I explored my surroundings, I realized no other women were present. This scared me, as my mother had told me what men sometimes did to young women. Fortunately, the men were indifferent to my presence.

"As I continued exploring, I found a narrow path that led away from the valley. I also observed an area with empty carts of various types. Some were being disassembled for firewood. There was a pile of nails and other metal parts. I surmised the carts had once belonged to kidnapped travelers. Judging by the large amount of metal, they took many travelers from the road. This answered some of my questions but left me frightened.

"I continued to explore, and I came across a metal cage with five people in it. One was a small girl. They all begged for their lives, and I tried to set them free, but the cage was secure. One of the men noticed my efforts and led me away. I spent the morning near the water, trying to perfect my ability to skip stones but I did not see Cleo during this time.

"I slept for the rest of the day, and when I woke up in the evening, I felt sick with no energy. I stood up and made my way to the circular area where the harvest had been done. The men began arriving, and they looked at me with quiet fascination. As the night wore on, my pain worsened, and something I could only describe as a drive built inside me.

"The men brought a Russian man from the metal cage into the circle and secured him to the same log from the previous night. Cleo appeared and took a commanding seat. She dressed in a lavish, white linen outfit with a magnificent gold crest on her head. This made her look like the snake she had used the previous night.

"The men circling the fire had started a slow chant and continued staring at me. I got the sense they were all waiting for me to do something, but I did not know what they were expecting. I began having a burning desire and thought strange, violent thoughts as the evening progressed.

"I had to see the Russian man. So I stood up and went over. He looked scared and said that his name was Uri and he was a traveler looking for work. These strange people had kidnapped him, and he did not understand why.

"I was not in the mood for conversation. Uri became frightened and begged for his freedom. He professed he was not a bad person and had done nothing wrong. He had a wife and two children. Our conversation was fascinating, but I had no interest in the topic.

"In time, a powerful urge took over my thoughts. I became convinced that I had to kill Uri. Horrified by this thought, I tried to fight my inner demon and resist the desire.

"The men brought several knives and placed them neatly on the table. Cleo walked over and pointed to the knives. She then looked at me and pointed to Uri. I had been staring at him, and he was becoming terrified.

"Eventually, my burning desire overcame all sensibilities, and I slit Uri's neck with the largest knife. Blood gushed all over my clothing, and Uri made a gurgling sound. Then, the men around the fire started chanting louder. One man would sing a single word, and then the next man would sing the same word, which went around the circle.

"Cleo pointed to the chest area, and I made a cut. I reached in and pulled out all the organs with my bare hands. I then cut out more of his organs with a different knife. It was common practice for me to gut animals as part of my chores, but the experience of cutting into a human was different. One man brought a tray, and I placed the bloody organs on it. I looked down at Uri's mutilated body. I knew he was dead but felt no emotion for my actions.

"Cleo said something, and the men stopped singing. She smiled and showed me how to cut the organs into smaller segments, then separate them into three ornate, bronze cups. This was frightening and oddly exciting.

"Cleo then showed me how to prepare the organs and the mint solution. She reached into a box and took out a black snake. Then she put the snake back into the box and motioned to me. A normal person would have been afraid, but I grabbed the snake. This was the first time I had ever touched a snake, and its scales felt strange. The snake hissed, but I kept a tight grasp near the animal's head. I was unaware that snakes could be deadly.

"Cleo showed me how to put a drop of venom into the cup. I followed her example, then put the snake back in its box. Cleo had set up a small mirror on a table, and she gave me a handheld mirror. Using the two mirrors, I was able to see my shoulder, and I used a knife to open my incision.

"Cleo helped me guide a spoon-like instrument inside the incision and remove the old pancreas from my shoulder. Then she showed me how to place the now-prepared pancreas into my shoulder. Finally, she watched as I used a needle and thread to stitch up my wound. My mother had taught me how to sew, and I performed this task well. A moment later, I nearly collapsed from exhaustion.

"The ceremony continued with different chants and throwing more gunpowder into the fire. The men encouraged me to dance, and I tried my best to emulate their dancing style while they shouted out what I thought were compliments.

"After dancing, I sat in a chair and looked at the dead Russian man. Before this event, Uri was alive, belonged to a family, and was in good health. Nevertheless, I was responsible for his death and felt awful. I wanted to cry or scream or beat my chest, but I was afraid of what the men might think, so I silently wept.

"I began walking around, first in meaningless circles. Eventually, I made it to the lake near the waterfall. In my despair, I got into the water up to my neck with my clothes on. The moon was bright, and I saw Uri's blood in the water.

"I stared at the water for a long time and then felt like I was being watched. I turned and saw Cleo behind me at the water's edge, wearing a look of contentment. She motioned for me to wash myself. Afterward, she handed me a cotton blanket. The water was dreadfully cold, and the night air did not help. Cleo led me to a cart that must have belonged to a traveler. The cart had straw in it, and Cleo motioned for me to go to sleep. I was used to sleeping in straw, so I quickly succumbed, covered by the blanket.

"When I awoke, it was dark, and I was unaware of how much time had passed. I found myself in the same traveler's cart. I noticed two fine horses tied up next to the cart. I sat up, and the first thing I thought of was my painful shoulder. I touched the wound; it hurt.

"I got out of the cart and see what the men of the camp were doing. As I stood, the first thing I noticed was that my headache from the night before was gone. I then noticed that overall, I felt well; better than ever. The air smelled remarkably fresh, and my night vision was incredibly vivid.

"When I walked around, I did not hear the men and realized I was utterly alone. The gypsy carts, men, Cleo, and horses were all gone. I made my way to the harvest circle, but the logs and rocks were moved into the forest. They even scattered the fire-ring ashes.

"I went back to the lake and stared at the water for several minutes. Then, I walked back to the cart, attached the horses, and climbed into the seat. I found a large, wooden, carved box under the seat. I almost opened it, but right away, I heard a hissing sound. I knew one or more snakes were inside.

"Next to the box was a bag that contained a small painted scroll. The moon provided enough light to see diagrams of human anatomy. Later, I studied it intently, and the diagrams offered instructions for the organ-harvesting procedures.

"On the other side of the scroll were several small pictures that seemed to repeat themselves in places. These pictures were like the ones on Cleo's gypsy cart. I concluded this was a language that used pictures instead of letters.

"Next to the bag, a ceramic vase held a plant that smelled like mint. Mint did not grow where I lived, so this was unique. There were also knives, cups, a needle, and thread.

"I saw no point in remaining in the camp, and I slowly drove the horses along the only trail visible. Although the moon was bright, it was difficult to navigate and hit many branches. The snakes hissed at every bump.

"An hour later, I came to the end of the thin trail, and there was a wall of trees. I got off the cart and explored. While the trees seemed dense, the men had carefully pruned one area so that a cart could pass.

"Just ahead was the dirt road I knew so well. I followed the road toward my house and stopped a hundred meters away.

"I did not know what to tell my family. So I sat in the cart and thought about my dilemma, and I decided not to tell them the complete truth. I did this for many reasons. At that time, the persecution of witches, while rare, did occur, and there was no doubt I would qualify. I was also deeply ashamed of killing that man. Plus, I did not wish to disappoint my father and mother. Taking a life was by far the worst thing anyone could do. Therefore, I hid the scroll, knives, cups, needles, and thread in the barn. I was naïve and hoped the scar would heal and the dreadful event would pass.

"When I arrived home late that night, my family was grateful to see me. My father and several other men had conducted an extensive search in the forest for five days but had found no trace.

"When they asked me where I had been, I told them gypsies capture me, and I was to be their slave. I made them believe I stole the gypsies' cart and injured my shoulder while escaping. Because I could not hide the two snakes and the mint plant, I showed them to my family. The two unusual animals and strange-smelling plants confirmed that gypsies were indeed involved. Everybody accepted this explanation, and my father was happy with two fine horses and a cart.

"The carved box had a male and female snake. My mother had looked at pictures of cobras before, and she told us they were dangerous and had to be treated with respect. So the snakes became family pets, and people would come from far away to feed them rats.

"My mother grew the mint plant indoors, and of course, they flourished. Mint leaves soon entered her kitchen, and our friends would request the sweet taste of her mint dishes or drinks.

"While my family was fine, I had survivor's guilt. I often woke up in a cold sweat, thinking of the murdered people. I would ask myself questions: *Why did they have to die? Why did I have to kill that man? Why couldn't I stop myself? Why was I chosen?* I struggled with these thoughts for many hours. At times, my family would have to wake me from a bad dream or find me crying for no reason.

"Even as I wrestled with my conscience, my body had never felt better or my mind sharper. I developed boundless energy, a deep sense of purpose and learned everything I could. My mother took a trip to her parent's house for books to keep me from asking her so many questions. I learned about history, mathematics, art, culture, and religion. I did not know how I would use this information or why I craved learning so much.

"Those around me could see a dramatic change. My family often talked about these newfound abilities. They assumed I was an exceptional child. But, inside, I knew that all of my greatness came from the harvest.

"After six months, the harvest effect lessened. The scar on my shoulder itched, and it hurt at night. One day, I realized the harvest needed to be repeated to maintain my abilities. This thought horrified me, and I certainly did not want to murder anybody.

"Searching for answers, I walked back to the lake where my transformation began. I skipped rocks into the water while struggling to find a solution to my problems. I knew I had the potential to be a successful person capable of significant contributions to society. However, this success would come at a substantial cost.

"I concluded that I must harvest, and this was the path I would take for the rest of my life. However, that explanation was not the whole truth. I knew I had boundless potential. My parents deeply instilled the trait of greatness in all of their children. We all had the powerful belief that it was our responsibility to accomplish much in this world. After many years of reflection, I would say that part of my decision to harvest was out of respect for the marvelous life my parents wanted me to live.

"The following day, I went into my father's forge and made restraints for holding a person. I had helped my father for years, and these restraints were of exceptional quality. I also got rope, a kitchen knife, my father's favorite hammer, and my mother's mirror. This mirror was one of her most prized possessions, and my uncontrollable desire to carry out my plan allowed me to ask permission to use it. I told her it was to scare birds; she did not like my idea but allowed me to borrow it.

"Supplies in hand, I then walked down the road to locate a perfect ambush spot. First, I prepared my rope and secured the restraints to a log. Next, I got a kitchen knife ready and waited for a traveler to come along.

"Soon, a cart with four horses and eight people appeared. I immediately realized my plan was poor. Looking at these innocent people made me feel mortified by my decision. They were ordinary travelers, and as I looked at their dreary faces, I became ashamed.

"I changed my decision, which provided a great sense of relief, but while I removed the restraints from the log, another cart appeared. I made a rash decision to go ahead. Upon reflection, the adverse effects of not harvesting had become increasingly intense, which was the most pronounced factor in my decision.

"A tired woman drove the cart, and I watched it slowly travel toward me. I concealed the kitchen knife and walked up to her. The woman looked exhausted, and she asked what they all ask: 'How far is it to Valdai?' As I answered, I was positioning myself to jump on the cart and attack her. Then I noticed she had a child. The sight made me feel awful, and I made a stronger vow never to harvest.

"I asked the child's name, and we had a pleasant conversation. While we spoke, an arrogant man rode up on a black horse and rudely interrupted us. He wanted to know if we had encountered a family of eight on the road. He explained that this family had ridden away during the night and owed him money. The woman said she had not come across anybody who matched that description.

"This rude man's attitude angered me. He seemed cruel and had no respect for women. So, once again reversing my vow not to harvest, I chose to take this man's life. I began by telling him the family he was seeking had recently passed through, and I would show him the way.

"The woman driving the cart went on her way, and I led the man to the forest, where I had made my preparations. Of course, I had to get the man off his horse, so I used the knife's broad side to slap the horse's rear end.

"The horse reared, and the man fell off. As he stood up, I thrust the kitchen knife into his neck. Unexpectedly, he stood up with the knife awkwardly sticking out. I was sure a large kitchen knife thrust through the neck would mean instant death. Unfortunately, he shouted an insult and chased me.

"We ran until he collapsed, at which point I stood over him and cried. I had killed a man for no reason. Yes, he was rude and was needlessly harassing a family about money. However, he had done nothing to me.

"I was going to walk away without harvesting, but the burning in my shoulder convinced me otherwise. So I followed the trail of blood back to his horse and tied it to a tree. Then I gathered my harvesting equipment and walked back to the man.

"I was still crying as I started the procedure. My efforts were crude, but I filled the three cups. I then applied the snake venom and mint mixture to the prepared organs. I propped the mirror in a tree and used one small knife Cleo had given me to remove the expired pancreas. I then prepared the new pancreas and placed it into my shoulder. It took great effort to sew up my wound with one mirror. Afterward, I felt better about my criminal deeds.

"When I looked down at the man, I wondered if I should say a prayer. It was then I noticed he had a leather pouch tied to his belt. I opened it to find more coins than my family had ever owned. I was about to take the money when I wondered if this theft was moral.

"I left the man with his money and said a brief prayer. Then, I took the man's horse and my harvesting equipment. On the way back, I washed in a stream. When I got home, I told my father I had found the horse. He said he would ask around to see whom it belonged to.

"That night, I could not sleep, but I felt better in the morning. It took significant soul searching to justify my actions, knowing I saved a runaway family from this cruel man.

"This became my pattern: every six months, I would walk along the road, pick out a traveler of ill repute, and harvest. I made the firm decision to only harvest bad people. It sometimes took a while, but I could always find a person who was cruel or dishonest. Gradually, my technique improved, and my fear subsided. I learned how to extract mint oil from the mint plant, and the two snakes had babies.

"The years went by, and I remained young while those around me grew old. I used the money from our family business to travel. Transportation was much slower, but I made my way through Russia, Europe, China, and India. Eventually, travel by ship became more acceptable, and I traveled to America, South America, Africa, Australia, Greenland, Iceland, and the Middle East.

"My family has long since passed away. I have some distant relatives, but it is obviously not possible for me to contact them. However, I return to my homeland often.

"Well, James, that brings us to the present. What do you think?"

"I have questions," I blurted out.

"They will wait until after dinner," Grace said with a warm smile.

EIGHT

We had talked the entire day, and it was now dusk. Usually, at noon, my body told me it was mealtime, and I had to eat something. However, I was undergoing several changes, and one of them was the lack of regular hunger pangs.

Inside the kitchen, Grace sat on a stool. There were no chairs here before, and I did not know where this one came from. She looked at me with a mischievous smile and said, "We will try your cooking."

This statement caught me off guard, and I asked, "First question: did you plan my cooking adventure this morning? Because I didn't see a stool here before."

Grace laughed and replied coyly, "Of course I planned it. Now cook. Chop, chop."

Her smile was infectious. I laughed and said, "Alright, but I am not that great a cook. I mainly do the prepared stuff like macaroni and cheese. When we did cook, my wife cooked, and I cleaned."

Grace grinned and said, "No excuses. If you need a cookbook, I have several. Also, your chopping skills need improvement."

I nodded, thought for a moment, and said, "Well, I know how to make lasagna, but we would need lasagna noodles, ground beef, tomato sauce, and cheese."

Grace shook her head. "How do you think the people in Italy made lasagna a long time ago? They just made it. Now let's get started. What's first?"

I did not know how to make the basic ingredients and guessed, "How about the noodles?"

Grace stood up and got flour, eggs, and salt. She poured out the flour on the table, cracked an egg into it, and added salt. She sat back on her stool and smiled, then motioned toward it. I did not know what to do, so I looked for some sort of noodle-making tool. Grace shook her head again. "Wash your hands, and then use your *clean* hands to mix the ingredients. You may add water as needed."

I put on an apron, washed my hands, and started kneading. Unfortunately, I spilled flour all over the floor, and Grace did not look happy. After some time, the gooey mess began looking like pasta dough.

Every so often, Grace threw in a dash of flour or improved my technique. Later, she got a rolling pin, and with great effort, I made a flat *thing* that I could cut up into two-inch-wide strips. Grace put the strips on a wire rack, set them aside, and then got back on her stool. Then, smiling and sounding amused, she said, "We have all night. What is next?"

I knew we needed pasta sauce, and that pasta sauce had tomatoes, and oregano, but that was the extent of my knowledge. So Grace and I headed for the greenhouse, where we picked tomatoes, onions, and oregano. Grace discreetly pulled out a garlic bulb, along with several other ingredients.

Back in the kitchen, I washed the tomatoes and began chopping. Grace sighed. "Normally, I would let you inadequately chop the vegetables, but there is a better way."

With a big grin, Grace reached under the main counter and pulled out a food processor. She plugged it into an outlet under the counter, and I processed the tomatoes.

The food processer was a European brand I had never encountered before, but it did a fantastic job. I soon added herbs, and it began looking like pasta sauce. Grace took out a large, cast-iron pot, and I poured the mixture in. Although the ingredients had not been cooked, they smelled magnificent.

Grace smiled and sat back down on the stool. I asked, "How about the cheese?" Grace pulled a commercial container of ricotta cheese and a block of mozzarella out of the refrigerator. I felt relieved that I did not have to milk cows and spend the night making cheese.

I laughed and said, "Alright, I wasn't expecting that. How about the olives?"

Grace got out a large Mason jar of olives and then sat back on the stool with her now-familiar "what's next?" smile. I asked, "Do you have any ground beef?" Grace pointed to a cooler next to the door.

The cooler was at room temperature, and this concerned me. Inside were several cuts of beef covered with slimy beef juice. She smiled and said, "Aged."

I pulled out a thick cut of beef that looked like a porterhouse steak. I cautiously sniffed it. The beef smelled delicious, like it was already cooked to perfection.

Grace reached under the counter and produced a hand-crank meat grinder. I cut up the steak and fed it into the grinder. The ground mixture was collected into a glass bowl. Then, without looking at Grace, I said, "I'm feeling a lot more comfortable around you."

Grace smiled again, and I asked, "Do you have many friends?"

Grace looked down, and I could tell that she did not. She fidgeted for a while and answered softly, "It is hard to get close to people as they pass away before your eyes. I prefer to meet people as I travel and not get close."

I wanted to ask her if she enjoyed eating meals with other people, but I could tell that she wanted to change the subject. So I found a large pot to boil the noodles and took out a pan to cook the ground beef. As the meat cooked, Grace threw in some spices and returned to her stool. I looked at her and asked, "How about dessert? Ice cream?"

Grace smiled and produced a small, hand-crank ice cream maker from under the counter. Then, I found some blackberries and fresh cream in the refrigerator. My mother had made ice cream like this when I was a child, and I kind of knew how to do it. As I was mixing the ingredients, Grace threw in salt, vanilla, and honey. She returned to her stool and looked at me with a thin smile. With the noodles and meat cooked, I got a large pan, assembled the lasagna, and put it in the oven. Grace surprised me by making garlic bread and setting the table.

It had taken three hours to make and cook the lasagna. Finally, we sat down to eat and our meal was by far the best I had ever made. It pleased me to watch Grace enjoying it. After dinner, we had a small amount of my tasty ice cream in cut-glass dessert cups. Between bites, Grace asked, "It feels good to enjoy your creations, yes?"

I smiled and nodded. Then we retired to the room with the large sofas. "What do you call this room?" I wanted to know.

Grace pondered this question for a moment and replied, "It serves as a study, art appreciation space, reading room, and place of contemplation. The term 'living room' would be suitable."

One minor question was answered, and I asked, "Would you like to continue our interview?"

Grace nodded, and I started my line of questions. "How does putting a pancreas in my shoulder make me live forever?"

"For one thing, you and I will not live forever," Grace answered with a smirk. "The body has a limit, and I am approaching mine."

It did not occur that there was a harvest limit, and suddenly I felt quite human. I was also surprised that Grace was gradually approaching her demise. She explained, "I have extensively studied the human body. Several years ago, I had a scientist investigate the harvest process using chemical analysis."

I interrupted, asking, "Was he a captive?"

Grace frowned and answered, "Of course he was a captive. He had plagiarized several studies, abused students, and stolen money from the university. Greed made him easy to manipulate.

"Once the scientist grasped the idea that he could live for all eternity, he worked nonstop to determine how the process worked, hoping he could commercialize the process. Eventually, he determined that a sustained immune system interaction was responsible.

"The pancreas is an immensely complex organ that produces many chemicals to regulate the body. When it is placed within a host body, the donor pancreas struggles to survive and sends out many chemical signals to prevent the host immune system from rejecting it. The host body counters this effort by sending out its own chemical signals. This results in an immune system arms race. The kidney-mint-oil solution acts as a moderator and prevents the host body from sending in white blood cells to attack the foreign object. In addition, the adrenal gland and snake venom solution sustains the pancreas by forcing the host body to provide nutrients.

"As the host body and donor pancreas interact, a remarkable side effect occurs. The host immune system begins a wide-spectrum fight that obliterates viruses, fungi, bacteria, dead cells, cancer, plaque, and scar tissue. In addition, the host cells get rejuvenated, so they are better prepared to fight off this foreign pancreas. As a result, the body is in perfect health, and the effects of age are subdued. In addition, this fight induces improved blood circulation, which allows your muscles and brain to function better.

"Do you remember your first urination after the harvest? The white material in your urine resulted from your body rejecting years of plaque. The harvest effect lasts until, eventually, the host body wins the fight and rejects the donor pancreas. When a new donor pancreas is introduced, the host body tries its old tricks to reject it, but they do not work, as this new pancreas is from a different person. A new fight begins, and the process is repeated. This interaction is vastly complex and cannot be replicated by any other method."

"Why in the shoulder?" I wondered.

Amused, Grace answered, "It took a long time for the scientist to unravel that mystery. The location for the donor pancreas is right between two muscles, next to a seemingly unimportant lymph node. A complex interaction takes place in that region. In addition, that area provides additional blood flow up to the neck, which helps the process. The big mystery is how this unusual process was conceived without modern scientific knowledge. That I cannot answer."

Grace took a long pause and continued, "I have put much effort into perfecting the harvest process, and it lasts up to eight months. After a body has aged like mine, the effect lasts two months. In time, my body will no longer put up a fight, and I will pass."

This was a lot to take in, and I asked a question to which I already knew the answer: "What happened to the scientist?"

Grace shook her head, and I assumed he was killed or harvested. She was such a private person she would never allow somebody with all her secrets to continue living.

"In eight months, I'll have to . . . *kill* somebody?" I needed to know.

"You will always have a choice," Grace answered. "You can live an extraordinary life or, after a short withdrawal period, your body will resume its normal aging process."

I had not realized I had a choice and that I could be normal. This news left me confused, and I took a moment to contemplate.

"I guess this is good news, and I can make this choice," I observed. But then I remembered my harvest experience. "Wait a minute. Then why did I go crazy after one day and kill that man? I was totally out of control. What was going on?"

Grace's mood changed. This often happened when I discussed an intelligent topic. She smiled and answered, "The host body is not used to fighting so hard and reacts aggressively. Essentially, your body was in a balanced state of shock. You must think of the body as a complex system. The body tries every possible trick to get back to what it considers normal. Because the fight is so taxing, the act of fighting becomes a normal state.

"Your body remembered how inserting the foreign pancreas made it healthy, and the immune system sent signals to your brain to force you to commit an unspeakable act. This is why you felt forced to harvest. Subsequent harvest will be less pronounced. With some strength, you can overcome this deep urge and live a normal yet short life."

This was a lot to take in. Grace talked about the rest of my life, but now the rest was not fifty years, but five hundred years. However, there was a confusing aspect. This whole topic was deeply personal, yet she wanted me to write a book about it. I did not understand why and changed the subject to find out. "You told me the harvest secret. If I write a book, anybody with a killer instinct will harvest. This would change the world. It will be a total bloodbath."

Grace smiled, leaned over, and spoke quietly, "I have given you and only you the complete understanding. For others to accomplish this task, it will require more than a verbal description. The pancreas must be prepared exactly as I have shown you. The slightest deviation will yield no results. The same is true of the kidney and adrenal glands. In addition, you do not know where to place the first incision. Only time will permit you to understand your anatomy well enough to make that critical incision.

"I also know that you will not provide a detailed anatomical description in your book. Your personality is such that you would never turn the world into a place of chaos. If a person wants to cut up bodies with mint and snakes, I cannot stop their choice. You may even skip a step when you write your book. I also know that if somebody finds you and tries to get this information out of you, they will fail. I know this because I have looked into your eyes."

I was not expecting such praise and found it gratifying that Grace had a high opinion of me. However, I did not get an answer to my fundamental question and asked, "Then why are you doing this? Why are you sharing your secrets with the world?"

Grace looked at her hands for a long moment. She had not done this for a while, and I knew I had hit a sore subject. Finally, Grace answered slowly, "If you do not know my reasons by now . . . well, then . . . I will tell you when we part ways."

We were going to part ways? I would not be with her forever? I guess this was good news. However, my core question went unanswered. I suspected it had to do with her leaving a legacy. I changed the subject. "As long as we are writing a book about your life, let's get some background information. Have you ever been married?"

Grace again looked at her hands for a long time, and I knew I had touched a deeply painful memory. I wished I could take back what I said.

"When I lived with my parents, I met a young boy on the road," she answered in a quiet, distant voice. "His horse was sick, and he had to stay with us until it got better. My confidence impressed him, and his good looks and warm heart captivated me. We were young and fell in love.

"We were married, but there were complications. I became pregnant, but my body fought the child, and I had a painful miscarriage. I was dreadfully sick for three months. That was the lowest point of my life.

"We were happy in each other's company. However, I never shared the harvest secret. His warm personality would never take a life, even if that life was vastly evil. I often think of his face, black hair, blue eyes, and strong arms that would hold me during a thunderstorm.

"In time, he grew old and passed. It was a core value to have a child, and I could not provide one. During our time, he never understood why I did not age. Every time he brought it up, I invented an excuse."

I found it noteworthy that Grace did not mention the man's name. She continued, "Over the years, I have been a foster mother and helped many families. So, in a way, I had many children. Twenty-two men propose to me, and I declined their offers because I could not bear to watch them suffer through the ravages of time. It is heartbreaking when people you care about pass."

"Would you ever consider a long-term relationship again?" I asked softly.

Grace shook her head, and I asked, "How about one date? Give a guy a chance to meet an older woman."

Grace laughed and answered, "I do not go out on what you would call dates, as I am a self-acknowledged complex woman. It would be as if I were dating a child.

"The people of today have lives that are full of wonder, and they are constantly in awe of learning some trivial fact that I knew three hundred years ago. But I do have a soft spot for artists and musicians. The true ones deeply appreciate life, and how to enjoy it."

"Do you miss it? The relationship part—having a partner, the arguments, the making up, the passion?"

"Of course. I would rather not have a lonely existence."

"Well, you could make one," I suggested.

Grace looked at me, puzzled, so I explained, "You could get twenty musicians and jam pancreases into them. Then, in a hundred years, pick out the best one."

Grace had a hearty laugh. "No, I do not think that would work," she said. "Musicians would forget to lock the door on the snake enclosure."

We both laughed for a long time. Afterward, Grace brought out a pot of tea, and I launched another round of personal questions. "Can somebody kill you?"

Grace gave me a "you asked another dumb question" look. "Of course," she answered. "The harvest process allows you to heal fast, but a major injury will take your life. I have been shot sixteen times, four of which were nearly fatal. Most of these occurred when I was taking a person for harvest, and a third party intervened. People have attempted to rob me, and of course, there are always wars."

This line of questions intrigued me, and I asked, "What was your worst injury? Or your top five?"

"Once, a butler, of all people stabbed all the way through my abdomen with a sword. He was protecting his master, who was in a coach. I nearly bled to death, but the harvest allowed me to recover quickly.

"I have been slashed at least forty times. Generally, in the arms or legs while struggling. I was stabbed twice in the heart. I thought I would die both times. Then, one day I woke up in a field. Somebody shot me in the head. I do not remember being shot or why it occurred."

I asked a question that had been bugging me. "What is the deal with your ears and nose?"

"This is an important topic. Our noses and ears are made of cartilage which continues to grow. Every thirty years, you must take care of this. Now they have plastic surgeons, but this is a recent occurrence. For many years, I had to operate on myself. Initially, the results were terrible, but I became skilled.

"Two weeks ago, I updated my nose and ears. I have tried plastic surgeons, but I do not think they do a good job. The harvest allows the scars to heal quickly. You should investigate good plastic surgeons. Incidentally, I have grown about one inch every hundred years."

This information was sobering. I liked my nose, and the thought of going under a knife was intimidating. I then thought about being five inches taller.

Now, Grace had a question for me. "What attracted you to Heather?"

"Well, she was cute and funny."

"Try again," admonished Grace. "Was it her legs, her face, her eyes, or the hot sex?"

Her sex comment really caught me off guard, but it made me stop and think. "You know, I enjoyed being part of a team. She had a plan, and I had a plan. We worked on improving our lives together. It was like we were always on the same page. But, that page was a fantasy."

"Is that why you pushed her out of your life so fast?" Grace asked with narrow eyes.

"Maybe," I admitted. "In retrospect, it wasn't the sleeping with Jake. It was the destruction of trust. We both knew she was never would be a successful fashion designer. But I appreciated her tenacity. I think that in the end, when I uncovered her big lie, it crushed me."

"And the hot sex?" Grace asked with a laugh.

"Hey, enough."

I knew she would not let up, and indeed, she kept prodding. "Well," I finally said, "We had a lot of fun. At least at the beginning, we were great together, physically; but after a year, it became routine. I still enjoyed it and, well, at least I think she enjoyed it. To answer your question, I do miss it. I miss being with somebody I trust and can have *hot sex* with."

Grace laughed and threw a pillow at me, and I felt we broke through a barrier and could be honest with each other. She smiled warmly, which made me feel comfortable.

I got up to stretch, and I noticed a compact disc in a hand-carved wooden case next to an intricate, stained glass miniature lamp. It seemed really out of place in this living room full of exquisite items. "What is the story behind this?" I asked.

Grace gave one of her now-trademark wicked smiles, got up, and retrieved both items, holding the miniature lamp in one hand and the compact disc in the other. She began in an authoritative voice, "This small lamp is a miniature Tiffany demonstration lamp that salespeople used before the Tiffany company became famous. I saved ten of them from being thrown away. Today there are three known miniature Tiffany demonstration lamps, and they have never come up for auction. I would estimate this lamp is worth two and a half million dollars."

Grace smiled and asked, "Do you still use compact discs for music?"

I shook my head but remembered that she had played one in the tow truck. "At its peak," she went on, "the compact disc sold for twenty-two dollars. The market was unprepared for when music distribution switched to computers. Record companies, music stores, and used CD outlets suddenly found themselves with what they considered worthless inventory.

"I sensed opportunity and began purchasing CDs at a substantial discount. The record executives could not believe their good luck. Often, they were so happy to unload their inventory that they would throw in pallets for free so they would not have to pay the disposal fees. I made deals with thrift stores and donation centers to buy their used CDs by the ton.

"I have been storing my collection in three large warehouses, and in five years, I will open an online store and three physical locations.

"To date, I have spent about $15 million on compact discs, which equates to approximately $3 billion of retail merchandise. It will take me several years to sell, but each year the collection increases in value. So, James, this is how you must think: long term.

"My first long-term investment was art. I became good at recognizing talented artists and bought their work when it was inexpensive. Not all art will become masterpieces, but a quality piece will retain its value.

"Today, there are many superb artists who produce excellent pieces. However, the new pieces do not appreciate like the old masters. In addition, the number of expert forgeries increased exponentially. This has caused the market to become diluted and untrusting. The sight of a forgery disgusts me, and this is why I now refuse to go to art museums. I do not see a future in art, and I am liquidating my collection."

Grace got up for a moment, stretched, and then sat back down. She looked at me and said, "I have two main business areas: shipping and accounting. These businesses are not exciting, but they are consistently profitable.

"I continue to invest, experiment, and expand. For example, one of my accounting firms was the first to use mechanical calculators, and another was the first to use computers. I commissioned the first steam and diesel cargo ships.

"A good, long-term opportunity you should consider is apartments. With apartments, you can start small and have steady growth. If you start conservatively, in a hundred years, you easily can amass a billion dollars."

A billion dollars? Me? Wow! I felt like I had won the lottery and blurted out, "Is that really possible?"

Grace could see the dollar signs flash in my eyes. "Yes," she answered impatiently, "That is what I took the time to explain."

I apologized for not showing the proper respect for her wisdom. "Please don't take my next question the wrong way," I added, "but I would like to know how much you are worth."

"In many cultures, this is a rude question," Grace chided, "and I take offense. However, I appreciate your attempts to gain knowledge, and I will answer.

"I have not done a recent calculation, but if you are looking for a number, it would be 1.2 trillion US dollars. Unfortunately, this is a misleading number, as the worth of an object can only be calculated after the sale.

I had never been in the presence of such a wealthy person. "Why have you tried so hard to make so much money?" I wanted to know.

Grace thought for a long moment and answered quietly, "As I have told you before, I was raised in humble surroundings. As a result, poverty was not a concern during my childhood. I had a wonderful time growing up with loving parents, brothers, and a sister. Of course, I occasionally encountered wealthy people on the road, but I was not envious.

"When I began harvesting, I traveled and started appreciating the finer things in life, especially art. My appetite required money, and I chose not to steal from those I harvested. My first business was an inn, like my parents. With this success, I expanded. The profit allowed me to purchase a large house and several dachas, or as you would call them, summer houses. My favorite one was on Lake Ladoga.

"I then concentrated on shipping and accounting. However, having wealth and maintaining wealth is unrelated. In the beginning, many people tricked me with 'sure thing' investments. In addition, I was naïve and tied my wealth to my real name.

"I became worried that if a harvest did not go well, I would have to leave my wealth behind. So I diversified my finances under different names. Over time, my wealth grew far beyond what I needed to keep comfortable. So it became a hobby as opposed to a necessity."

This was a fantastic look into Grace's past, but I wanted to know more. "What do you spend your money on?"

Grace thought for a moment and then answered, "I used to desire large houses on vast properties. Fulfilling my dream included the best servants, artists, cooks, trainers, and all manner of people at my beck and call. However, I found my life to be less stressful without people and expensive possessions surrounding me.

"I occasionally spend money for fun. One of my guilty pleasures is to turn stories into plays or movies. Did you watch the movie *Ben Hur*?"

I nodded, and Grace continued, "I enjoyed reading that book, so I invested in making it into a play and then a successful film. They recently made the story into a new movie, but I have no desire to watch it. Of course, if you look into the history of *Ben Hur*, you will not find my involvement."

Grace paused for a moment and then said, "This does not answer your fundamental question. The money I freely spend goes to scholarships. I have several foundations that seek out students who meet specific criteria. These are creative youngsters who cannot afford college. The last time I checked, 30,000 students were receiving partial or full scholarships from my investments."

That answer prompted another question. "Do you give out scholarships because you feel guilty about your harvest victims?"

"I give out scholarships is to make the world a better place. As far as guilt, a proper harvest will make the world a better place, so there is no guilt."

I still wanted to know more. "Do you ever give money to the families of the people you harvest? I mean, sometimes you are taking away their only income source."

That question made Grace uncomfortable. "Yes, this is true. I have taken away a family's only income source. But, when I do, I make sure that they are provided for."

"How?"

"Various ways. I have given their children scholarships or had my corporations hire family members. I prefer not to give out money because this often leads to laziness and objectionable moral values." Grace shifted in her chair and continued, "What you may not realize is that when you take an evil element out of society, the wound will heal. For example, an abusive father. At first, the family is sad, but they realize their lives are much better without his anger and cruelty. They flourish because they are no longer repressed. Often the mother or children will find jobs and are much happier without a bad father's 'help.'

"Two years ago, I harvested the father of a family with two children. The husband was a foul beast who served as an enforcer for a loan shark. The morning I harvested him, he had broken the jaw of an eighty-year-old father in a wheelchair to send a message to the delinquent son.

"After the harvest, the mother got a job at a beauty salon, began dating, and married a construction foreman. She recently posted on Facebook that they are expecting another child. If you look at her Facebook pictures from years ago, they were dreary. Now her Facebook pictures have big smiles."

I really needed to change the subject and asked, "Do you have a will? What will happen if you die?"

"That question has a complex answer," Grace said. "Since I will still be alive for some time, I do not have a will. A traditional will would be out of the question because my corporations are under many names. When I get closer to my passing, I will disperse my investments. They will go to various charitable foundations. However, if I were to pass today, the decisions would be chaotic, as all the corporations overlap. I suspect that the ultimate decision would be in the courts for a hundred years."

Grace smiled as if watching a hundred years of legal fighting from heaven would be fun. Then, I changed my tack and queried, "What do you think your greatest contribution has been?"

Grace thought for a long moment and answered, "That is a good question. I have helped many people, employed millions, and made the world a better place by getting rid of undesirable people."

That answer struck a negative chord, and I challenge, "Undesirable? Is that how you see them?"

"Of course," Grace replied. "They are evil people who feed on the good of society!"

"But," I protested, "we have an entire court system with laws, judges, and defense attorneys. You bypass all of that and pronounce your own harsh sentence. I mean, they never have the chance to defend themselves!"

Grace looked at her hands for a long moment and offered, "Yes, this is true. I have taken the lives of many people who had not committed what the average person would call a 'substantial crime.' You do not see the effect that an evil person has on a community over his or her lifespan. One bad person is like an untreated infection. It grows, causes pain, and eventually ends in death.

"Evil people promote more evil people, and their effect goes on for generations. You can see it in a family, business, or community that has an evil member. In every case, it can be traced back to a single person. After they are removed, the rebuilding process begins, and, in time, the community and family are better off. I understand you do not see this now, and I know the laws of our society do not accept my harsh actions.

"Having lived as long as I have and having observed the vast amount of destruction a single bad person can cause. I can honestly say I have made the world a better place, one person at a time."

This logic actually made sense to me. It then occurred to me that my harvest might affect my judgment. I wondered if my internal "moral compass" had shifted. I wanted to get back to the personal aspect of harvesting and asked, "What do you feel for those whose lives you have taken?"

"Absolutely nothing! They were bad people!"

Grace looked angry. I waited for a moment and asked, "Did you ever harvest a person who wasn't bad?"

Grace looked at her hands for a long time before answering softly, "Over my lifetime, I have taken many innocent lives. My first was a small girl who unexpectedly came upon me as I was harvesting her father. She began striking me with her little fists. I pushed her away without intending to hurt her, but she fell backward and fatally hit her head. I felt sad for a long time over this unfortunate incident.

"Over the years, I have taken many lives I should not have. Many of them were good people who attempted to rescue my harvest subject. I can usually stun an innocent person, but often their good deed led to their demise. I feel sad when this occurs. While you may not understand this now, taking a good life in the service of removing evil people is worth the price. I have not had an unintended death since 1919.

"To formally answer your question, there was only one occasion where I harvested an innocent person. I was opening the window of a warlord's house when a guard surprised me."

I really wanted to change the subject, so I asked a lighter question. "Have you harvested somebody famous?"

"It is interesting that you should ask that question," Grace said, looking amused. "I have harvested several political figures and religious leaders. They were important in their day, and if you did a careful search, you would locate a record of their passing. I can only think of one person who was of great consequence. He was the first cousin of Ivan Vasilyevich or, as you would call him, Ivan the Terrible. This man was brutal and dispensed punishment for no reason. I made his death look like an accident, and those around him did not mourn his passing."

I thought about this answer and then said, "I think that I'm getting a picture of who you are, but from my perspective, you are two people. One does unspeakable acts, and the other is a pleasant person."

Grace smirked and said, "You have an amusing method of asking questions. I may appear to be two different people from your perspective. On the one hand, I am a person who commits 'unspeakable acts,' as you put it, and a refined woman. Yes, I can see how this could be viewed as confusing. I will therefore clarify this misconception. I understand that you have never spent time on a farm?"

I nodded, and Grace continued, "Life has a different meaning on a farm. A farmer watches the birth of an animal, the animal maturing, plays with the animal, and then takes the animal's life for meat. That is the cycle of life. This does not mean I do not hold human life in high regard. However, farm life provided a deep understanding of where our place is.

"I treated you the same way I would treat any harvest subject. I have learned to keep my guard up, and the harvest subject must know his or her place.

"This is the same I would treat a farm animal. First, one must be firm and then reward good behavior. In this area, humans are very similar to horses. Like a horse, once you had proven to be more trustworthy, I treated you better."

I did not like being compared to a horse, and Grace continued, "In the small circle of people I interact with, the next layer up would be my employees. I've found that the best way to treat an employee is 'tough, but fair.' Together we work out mutually acceptable goals, and then I receive status reports on how these goals are accomplished. On occasion, I acted too harshly and corrected my actions.

"My next level would be those whom I socialize with. For example, I occasionally attend plays and concerts. When I get together with these people, I act friendly and go to great lengths to be pleasant. However, I am never the life of the party.

"Have the people you socialize with ever been to this house?"

Grace shook her head. "Do you have a level of people above that?" I asked. "Like a close friend? You know, somebody you can have 'girl talk' with?"

Grace had turned away, and I said softly, "You should probably work on getting some close friends."

Grace nodded without looking at me. "Well, what do you think of me now?" I asked. "Am I a horse, or did I make it to employee?"

Grace laughed and answered, "You have potential."

"Not really an answer. How do you really feel about me?"

I understood I had entered untested waters. Grace paused, collecting her thoughts, then replied quietly, "You have a good heart. However, you have a lot to learn about yourself and how to treat the people close to you."

"And that makes me what? A friend?" I challenged.

"A colleague. Yes, that is an appropriate answer."

This "answer" sent chills up my spine, so I shifted to a new topic. "Were you ever caught or punished for a harvest?"

Once again, Grace looked at her hands, and I could tell I had hit a sore subject. I wished I could take that question back.

Grace looked away, then down at her hands again, and said in a labored voice, "The authorities apprehended me many times, but I quickly escaped. However, there was one painful exception.

"I was in a small, secluded cabin harvesting a murderer. Russia was in a state of political transition, and this region was forming an army. A group of ten soldiers came into the cabin looking for people to join the army, and they apprehended me.

"There were no trials, but I convinced the army that the opposing side forced me to punish people. Fortunately, the soldiers agreed to spare my life and sent me to prison. As the only woman, the men treated me poorly. I knew how to fight, but fending off over a hundred men proved impossible.

"During my incarceration, I could not harvest, became terribly sick, and aged irregularly. It took me eight months, but I convinced a guard to lead me to a secluded spot with the promise of sex. I snapped his neck, exchanged clothes, and walked out the front gate.

"After my escape, I went back to the cabin. Fortunately, my mint oil was present, but the snakes had died. So I went home, and my brother's great-grandson had four snakes on display. So I pretended to be a traveling salesperson and purchased two. Otherwise, the nearest cobra was many months' travel, and I was in no condition to make the journey.

"After my recovery, I learned all I could about self-defense. In addition, I have studied the human body in great detail to understand the weaknesses and nerve points. I also mastered every type of weapon and keep at least four on me at all times. You observed weapon number one in the kitchen.

"Since then, I never allowed myself to stay captured. One of my greatest powers is the art of appearing defenseless."

I was holding onto a question and decided this was the right time to ask, "What do you want to tell the world? I mean, you have a lot of wisdom. What would you like to share?"

I was surprised when Grace frowned and answered, "I have observed people for many years, and they rarely accept unsolicited advice."

I probed deeper, "What *should* we be doing?"

"A person can be good, bad, or indifferent, but together people form a community, which forms a city, which forms a state, which forms a country. Each of these groupings has a unique personality and reflects the individuals.

"There are many trends in modern society, with television and the Internet reaching all regions of this planet. A person can make a video of their cat sneezing, and by the next day, a billion people have witnessed it. Yet slavery, state-sponsored corruption, death camps, suicide bombs, mass murders, hate cults, and horrific crimes have become acceptable to the masses. When people feel overwhelmed, they change the channel.

"This morning, there was a suicide bomb in an African town square, with twenty-six people killed. This was a great tragedy for the families. Yet this horrific incident was not in any major United States news outlet. So if you are looking to me for a message or wisdom that spans my extensive life, I have nothing to offer."

Grace paused for a moment and added, "This is a beautiful world. Enjoy it, respect it, respect others, and respect yourself."

This was fantastic wisdom, but not the answer I was searching for. I felt Grace was acting cagey and I probed deeper. "Have I upset you?"

Grace looked at her hands for a moment and then realized what she was doing. She looked up and answered, "No, you have not."

Grace looked away, and I resisted speaking to allow her to think. Eventually, she turned back and said, "This experience is more uncomfortable than I had expected. As you know, you

are the first person to know my actual past. In normal conversations, I ask the questions. Your last question about the
world, for example. I provided a terse answer, and I regret this.

"If another person without your knowledge asked that
question, I would have lightheartedly responded. However, my
answers will reach a wide audience. Therefore, I will try to be
more forthcoming. Please ask another question."

Glad we were back on track, I asked, "Where do you see
society going?"

Grace looked at me for a long moment and then got up.
When she returned, she was carrying two small objects. One
was a McDonalds Happy Meal toy, and the other was an old
cast iron toy of a boy on a horse. I noticed one of the horse's
legs was broken, and it was rusty.

Grace looked at me for a long moment and said, "When I
was forty-five, a nearby town began building a church. The
town employed fifteen to twenty-five craftsmen. Mainly stone
carvers and carpenters. The town hired an architect to oversee
the project. He was a talented man who laid out his plans on
a slate he carried with him. The church took fourteen years
to build. There were a few setbacks, but this was the typical
build time of such a structure.

"As the church was being built, the townspeople would
often gather and watch the progress. Then, when the structure was complete, they had a weeklong celebration. Today,
people still marvel at this opulent structure, even though it is
hundreds of years old.

"Two years ago, I visited one of my accounting firms near
Boston. I noticed a surveyor working in an empty parcel of

land. I returned six months later and an office building occupied the lot. It was much larger than the church I described.

"The building was typical of what you would expect. It was flashy on the outside and drab on the inside. They had put up a 'now leasing' sign. I returned recently, and the building was still vacant.

Grace suddenly changed the subject, "Describe the object in your right hand."

Remembering our recent conversation about objects appreciating over time, I answered, "It is an antique cast iron horse that's worth much more than you paid for it. It's probably a children's toy."

"Describe the object in your left hand."

"It's an inexpensive Happy Meal toy."

"Which is better crafted?"

"The horse is made out of cast iron and hand-painted. It is obviously much better in quality."

With a crafty look, Grace asked, "What point am I trying to make?"

"That they used to make things better in the old days."

Grace shook her head and said, "You have been paying attention, but not enough. What you have in your right hand is the old-time equivalent of a Happy Meal toy. In 1921, a dry goods store had 100 of these made to give out to their best customers. I kept this example as a reminder of the owner, whom I knew well.

"Look at the paint; it is sloppy around the eyes, saddle, and legs. Now look at the cast-iron mold lines; they were not ground down before painting. The cast iron was of inferior quality, and thus, the leg broke.

"Now, look at the Happy Meal toy; it's a sturdy, well-de-signed product. The colors are perfect, and there is extensive detail. It even lights up blue when a child makes a noise. On a higher level, it is an excellent facsimile of the movie character it represents. Your left hand holds an astounding achievement of marketing and technology. What you have in your right hand is a poor example. What does all that tell you?"

I had never considered how impressive a disposable Happy Meal toy could be. Then, I looked closer and, the toy contained a lot of detail, and it was well-crafted. I looked at the cast iron horse, now clearly seeing the defects. Still, I was not sure what answer she was expecting. "I don't understand. Does this mean we're making progress as a society?"

Grace sat back, stared at me for a long moment, and she said, "You asked me about my perspective for where society is going. To formally answer your question, society is moving much faster in all aspects and accomplishing much more.

"The increase in speed has caused our society to make some compromises. For example, the fresh pasta you made. It tasted better than dry pasta for two reasons. The first is that you made it from scratch from quality ingredients, and the second was that you appreciated all your hard work. Society has traded that handmade pasta for instant, dried pasta. In this trade, society got an inexpensive product with a long shelf life and an endless variety of shapes and flavors. The tradeoff is diminished taste.

"From this, we see that society is doing more at a faster pace, and the people do not appreciate what we have. For example, we have many television channels we never watch.

I clearly remember the anticipation to get *a single* television channel. Incidentally, when that channel arrived, it only had four hours of programming per day.

"I see this fast trend accelerating. For example, robots will build office buildings. As a result, they will complete the structure in two months with robot precision quality. A future Happy Meal toy will walk and talk. Keep in mind that the goal of the Happy Meal toy is a brief moment of disposable entertainment.

"The conclusion that I draw is that society is fast becoming a brilliant child with a short attention span."

This was a stunning revelation, and I took a moment to appreciate her insight. Then, I continued on a positive note. "Wow, that's a wonderful analysis. But now, I want to know more about the past. You have witnessed so much over your lifetime. What is the most amazing historical event you were a part of?"

As soon as I ended my sentence, I knew I had botched it from the look on Grace's face. "What you forget," Grace reminded, "is that the world has changed. Information spreads instantly. When new lands or marvelous inventions were discovered, I was completely unaware. For example, I found out about the telephone twenty years after it was invented.

"I have been present at significant moments of history, met people who were famous in their day, met people who would become famous, listened to great works of music, and observed the beginnings of amazing endeavors.

"However, it is only in recent times that we can put a context to these situations. In addition, it is only now possible for us to appreciate famous events in the present. For example, I appreciated the Challenger space shuttle explosion was an important event.

"To formally answer your question. Hmm . . . the telegraph radically changed the world. Suddenly we got news of faraway events the same day they occurred. It was an astounding achievement that changed many lives forever.

"As far as significant people, let's see . . . Benjamin Franklin and Wolfgang Mozart were more impressive than history gives them credit. They were also quite charming.

"That still does not truly answer your question. I was in Paris before World War I. At that time, the city was an upbeat, happening society. The center of world culture. The people were so . . . *progressive*. The entire town felt . . . *electric,* and everybody knew it. I could not wait to get out of bed in anticipation of having a great day. I miss what Paris used to be, and history did not properly record that time period."

"What religion are you?" I wondered to know.

Grace sighed and answered, "All religions follow the same pattern. A person or small group starts a religion with good intentions. They accomplish this task by taking good ideas from other religions, adding their own spin, and reorganize them. If these people do a good job of promoting their religion, other people get behind this 'new' idea, and it becomes popular.

"The religion then changes to say 'all other religions are bad.' New leaders get appointed and covet their power. Then, the religion becomes twisted and corrupt, which upsets the followers. Soon, the cycle begins again. It is a travesty that people do not recognize this simple pattern.

"You will find this same pattern in politics, literature, companies, entertainment, music, and art. To formally answer your question, I was raised Russian Orthodox, but I no longer practice. At times, I say an Orthodox prayer.

"Hmm. That answer does not fully answer your question. I find Buddhism interesting."

I wanted to know more about her life choices and asked, "Do you regret going into that forest?"

Grace thought for a moment and then answered, "I would have married, had several children, lived to an old age, and then passed away. Not going into that forest would have spared me the horror of harvesting and watching those around me wither away. However, I would not have seen the many wonders of the world or known so many wonderful people.

"You know, I would not have met you, either. But, to formally answer your question: yes, I would have gone into that forest knowing what I now know."

"But would you recommend it to others?" I wanted to know.

Grace's expression became fierce. "Absolutely not!" she retorted angrily. "I have only converted you out of necessity! I did this to capture my story with complete clarity."

Taken aback by her angry outburst, I asked quietly, "But this makes you alone."

Grace nodded, and I really needed to change the subject. "Did you ever meet Cleo after your first encounter?"

Grace walked to a shelf and showed me an ornate, solid-black stone bust that depicted an attractive woman. "Do you recognize her?" she asked.

I shook my head, and Grace continued, "This bust is of the Egyptian pharaoh Cledopart or, as you would pronounce it, Cleopatra. This is the woman who performed my first harvest."

The Cleopatra? Wow! However, this revelation made sense. Only a person of authority and an obsession with beauty could invent something so outrageous.

"Our paths have not crossed since our first meeting," Grace continued, "I applied significant effort to locate her over the years without success."

"Why do you think she chose you?" I wondered.

Grace answered softly, "I have asked myself this question many times. I still do not fully understand her reasoning, but in meeting you, I understand some of her logic. It may have been for the same reason that a mother wants a child. In other ways, the answer is more complex. Honestly, you can get bored over five hundred years. Perhaps it is like planting a tree and waiting to see what the fruit will taste like. I will keep an eye on you."

Another giant concept I would have to think about for the next hundred years. *Wait! Did I just think in terms of a hundred years? Did I give myself permission to harvest?*

I needed to get my head back into the game. "Have you encountered any other people who know how to harvest?"

"My accounting firms have done careful economic searches for people like myself, and their results are inconclusive. It is difficult when generations of families share the same business. To that result, I have uncovered a few wise people whom I suspected knew the secret, but this lead proved to be false."

"If you met a harvester, what would you talk about?" I wondered.

"How about five hundred years of history?" Grace answered with a hearty laugh. "We would surely have a long conversation about our lives and how we learned the secret of the harvest."

A question popped into my head, "Is there a term that differentiates you from other people? Like a harvester?"

Grace did not look happy. "I dislike labels. I am a woman, and that is the only term which applies."

I got the sense that, once again, I had upset Grace. Finally, she got up and said, "It is getting late, and there is still much to discuss. We should retire for the evening."

I agreed, then finished my now cold tea and went to my room. I again found a neat arrangement of clothing. I had been with Grace the entire day, and still I wondered how she made these piles of clothes appear without leaving my sight. I took a shower and changed into stylish striped pajamas.

When I entered the bedroom, I saw something under the covers. I carefully peeled them back, and Heathcliff looked up at me. Unsettled, I slowly put the covers back and walked out of the bedroom. Grace turned the oil lamps down to a small flame. I went to each door, knocked softly, and whispered, "Excuse me," and then waited for an answer. One of them produced a result, and the door cracked open.

"Yes?" asked Grace.

I could tell she was annoyed. "Umm, Heathcliff . . ." I stammered.

Grace nodded, closed the door, and then a few minutes later, opened the door and stepped out. She dressed in a silk nightgown that was clearly custom-fit. I noticed elaborate, colorful rose-themed embroidery around the shoulders, and I wondered if she had made it.

We went to my bedroom, and she shoved Heathcliff off the bed. Heathcliff landed on the floor, gave Grace a defiant look, and returned to the bed while staring at me. Grace shook her head and said, "She wants to sleep here, and baby gets what baby wants. So you will just have to sleep with me."

Astonished, I told myself to get a grip. *When you were eight, you slept with your sister in the same bed, which is the same thing.*

We stopped in the kitchen, and Grace got some oils and other items out of the cupboard. She mixed them together with a mortar and pestle. Grace then used a rubber bulb to suck up the mixture. She looked at me with a mischievous smile and said, "This will hurt."

I did not understand what was going on. Suddenly, Grace grabbed me by my hair, bent my head back, and with two quick jabs, she sprayed the mixture up my nose. She then forced me over near the sink.

I coughed and wheezed. My eyes teared up, and I tried to talk, but I could not. One ingredient must have been chili oil, and it burned after I blew it out. It took time, but my head cleared. Grace gave an evil smile and taunted me: "Now, you will not snore."

Between gasps, I said in a tight voice, "You could've warned me!"

Grace laughed and walked away. I followed her, curious about her bedroom. I assumed it would be Victorian-meets-MTV. The door opened, and it was rather spare compared to the other rooms. The queen-sized bed was neat, with an intricately designed bed cover. Her furniture theme was European modern with light, finished wood. There were three dressers, a large mirror, and a walk-in closet. The only decoration was a painting on the wall. I recognized Grace as the girl in the painting and suspected that the other people were her family.

Grace smiled and got into bed; she was on the left side, facing up. I slid under the covers and tried to relax. I was still wheezing and spoke quietly: "My face is feeling better. How do you know about this treatment?"

Grace whispered a reply, "It is an ancient African folk remedy. The treatment will last for one week. You may get closer if you wish."

Electric shocks ran through my body. Grace was attractive, and I could see myself falling for her. On the rare occasions when she laughed, the room brightened. However, this extraordinary woman had torn a man open, murdered him, and then encouraged me to do the same. She also owned a mountain lion and had recently pointed a gun at my face.

These negative thoughts quickly put a damper on my libido. Yet I had to respond and played it cool. I carefully moved closer, so my shoulder touched her shoulder. We were both staring at the ceiling. In the dim oil lamp light, I noticed hundreds of tiny, reflective specks on the ceiling. It suddenly hit me that I could make out the Big Dipper; the specks were in the pattern of the stars. I carefully pointed to them with my left hand. I could tell Grace was happy I noticed this detail, but she did not speak.

We were both relaxed, and I knew that the next move was mine to make. *How cool would it be to get intimate with a five-hundred-year-old woman?* Grace probably knew every sexual position ever tried. However, another part of me remembered her flopping me onto a wooden board with one arm and then strapping me down. So I decided to play it safe.

With a lot of bravery, I whispered, "Umm, roll over, please."

Grace hesitated and then complied. In my mind, I was sure that she had one hand on a gun, a knife, or a James Bond eject-author-through-the-roof button.

I began to lightly massage her back with my right hand. My efforts seemed to be acceptable, and I felt more comfortable. Next, I changed my motion to work her neck and lower back. I took great care to avoid the shoulder incision or any intimate region. I did not apply too much pressure and kept my movements slow.

The skin on her neck felt smooth, and I was on the verge of enjoying the experience. I often gave Heather a back rub like this when I had inadvertently upset her and wanted to get out of the doghouse. To me, this move meant, "I'm not admitting fault, but I am sorry you are upset. (Without actually saying sorry.)"

At first, Grace was tense, but she relaxed. I kept up the pace and targeted her problem muscles while remaining extremely careful. I could tell she had a nice body, and I was sure she worked out. A good masseuse can tell a lot about a person. If I were to summarize, I would answer: complex, but tender.

The experience made me wonder how I actually felt about Grace. I wondered if I could get emotionally close to her and if she would allow herself to open up enough to allow a relationship. I also wanted to know what she thought about me and this experience.

I had allowed myself to relax, and it felt gratifying to be with her. However, after fifteen minutes, I knew something was going terribly wrong. I was not sure if I had taken things too far or not far enough. While I was trying to figure this out, I realized Grace was softly crying.

I did not know why or what I had done to sadden her. I started to ask but the voice in my head screamed: *Do not ruin this moment with useless talk. Finish up and say good night.* Usually, my little voice does not provide the greatest advice, but it had been spot-on the last few days. I wondered if the harvest effects improved my little voice. I finished up and whispered, "Good night, Grace."

NINE

I woke up, and Grace was still under the covers. I reasoned I had slept with a five-hundred-year-old, kind-of-cute mass murderer. What is the proper way to say good morning— "Good morning, sweetie?" I played it safe and asked, "How was your sleep? Did I snore?"

There was no response. I slowly got out of bed and briefly thought about riffling the drawers but knew that would be a fatal mistake. I stretched, and the door unexpectedly opened. Grace popped her head in to announce, "Heathcliff tossed me out of bed at around three. She really has a thing for you. I still have not figured out how she opens the doors. I will have to use a camera on her one of these days."

The statement took me aback, I looked back at the bed and Heathcliff. I swear this big cat was grinning her fang-filled mouth at me. I spoke sarcastically, saying, "Good morning, ladies."

Then, in a moment of pure bravery, I scratched Heathcliff on the head. Her hair felt like a stiff brush, and she seemed to tolerate this action or enjoy it. *How do you read the emotions of a mountain lion?* Graced chuckled and left the bedroom.

I cleaned up and got dressed. This time, it was a navy-blue ensemble in a neat pile beside the bed. Grace dressed in a modern outfit—a toned-down steampunk waitress, meets '80s-power-female-executive. Her look was unique but completely classy.

We had a tasty breakfast of poached salmon with capers and dill. I watched Grace cook, and she used normal ingredients without fanfare. I still could not understand how something so simple could taste so good. Our conversation was light, as I did not know how she would react to sleeping with me. I got the feeling the subject was off-limits.

After breakfast, we walked around the yard and inside the barn. It was a beautiful day for a short stroll. Back in the living room, I got my *Dawson's Creek* notebook, which I rescued from a Best Buy trash pile. It was almost full, so I mentioned, "I will need some more paper soon." Grace reached into a drawer and produced an identical Dawson's Creek notebook. Either she had been planning this for years, or she was that good. I suspected she was *that good.*

Getting down to business, I began, "I wanted to get some more background on your emotions, convictions and . . ."

Grace unexpectedly cut me off, "You need to be prepared. As a young girl, I was not. Let's discuss selecting the person you are going to harvest. This person must be far away from where you live. They must never recognize you. A good rule is a two-hour drive.

"To find this person, start with the part of town that breeds corruption. You would think poor areas, drug houses, jails, and homeless parks would be ideal, but this is incorrect. You must start where people gather and are supposed to be safe and happy. Start with churches, schools, playgrounds, coffee shops, music clubs, shopping malls, museums, city halls, or sporting events.

"You must open your mind and observe. People will enjoy themselves—laughing, singing, praying, learning, working, and appreciating life. Observe this pattern and look for the negative—the raised voice or curse words. This will lead you to a person, and you will observe them. Often, they will lead you to another and, eventually, you will locate the source.

"When you have identified the truly evil person, you must discreetly get to know them and find out their routine. The Internet now speeds up the process. However, you must plan carefully and never use your own computer to investigate. When you are sure this person is a prospect for a harvest, determine how to meet them without arousing suspicion. For example, you might dress up as a delivery person and ask for a signature.

"Look into their eyes. The eyes hold the key to the soul, and you must learn how to read eyes. A person can look evil, but in reality, be difficult, different, or mentally damaged. I have met many arrogant, apparently awful people who had wonderful, warm hearts. But, as with all people, their eyes will reveal the truth. I knew the moment I first looked at you what kind of person you were."

I felt a pronounced chill in my spine as Grace continued, "Your eyes told me you had great potential, but you were lazy and distracted. Your eyes now tell me you have some focus and a glimpse of purpose.

"Once you have selected the harvest person, much work is to be done. First, select the time and place of the abduction. The most important part of the location is your safety. It needs to have multiple exits, good visibility, places for concealment, and be free of people. In addition, look for security cameras and places where hidden people might observe you.

"All of your equipment must be present so that you can restrain your harvest, silence them, and defend yourself. Bring at least two false identities that do not lead back to you. The Internet now makes this task simple and inexpensive.

"You must dress in such a way that you do not look out of place and cannot be later identified. If you recall, my hair was uncombed, and I had a noticeably dramatic appearance.

"Once you have secured your harvest, remove any evidence of the abduction. Often a harvest will drop something during the struggle. Fingerprints, hair, cloth, and even shoe prints can lead to you. It is essential to turn off cell phones, pagers, and computers. You must also secure the person's car. Cars now have location technology that must be disabled. The authorities look for cars more carefully than people.

"Before the abduction, a plan with several contingencies must be in place for disposing of the body. A missing body is not acceptable, and the authorities will continue the search for years. Never try to disguise the body; this will increase investigation attention. Do not think that you can bury or burn a body and then walk away. With modern crime investigation techniques, this is the worst mistake.

"Ideally, authorities will locate the body within six hours after the abduction. This will limit the investigation scope. The fingerprints and face should never be obscured. The harvest victim's identification and personal possessions must always be present to limit the scope.

"The death must have an apparent cause not related to a harvest. It needs an obvious path that never leads to you. A mystery death like a fire, suicide, accident, hate crime, car crash, or explosion is not acceptable. The authorities will always look deeper, and they may notice a pattern even if there is no pattern. You do not want them to identify you by mistake.

"In all cases, the authorities will conduct an extensive investigation that included an autopsy. This information will be entered into a computer database. Once entered, it cannot be removed. The data might reveal a pattern, and then a task force will be formed. The task force will link with international databases and other task forces.

"You must not allow a task force to form, as it will bring attention to old crimes. These old crimes are not related to you, but the undeniable links will justify an enlarged task force.

"Getting back to the harvest. It leaves precise incisions on the body, along with burn marks. A good autopsy will record the anomalies, and therefore you must disguise your incisions or clearly explain their presence. A good disguise is a gunshot, knife wound, or animal bite. When I used the soldering iron, I kept the damage to the belly. I have tried to use electricity as a torture instrument, but it proved less effective.

"Let me give you a sample harvest: A local store owner is forcing his female employees to have intimate relations. This is a start, but you must make sure everything is as it appears to be. Some men naturally attract women, and women do, occasionally, make mistakes. While a pattern of torrid affairs may seem dishonest, there may not be a negative element, coercion, or the pleasure of inflicting pain. In all cases, you must see the evil in their eyes. If you do not, then their death will haunt you. James, I have looked into your eyes, and you are not strong enough to overcome the guilt of killing an innocent person.

"After you have confirmed this person is indeed worthy of a harvest, you must pick an abduction place. A suitable location would be in the store's parking lot. Then, after checking for security cameras, develop a reason to make the harvest work late.

"In the parking lot, use a Taser with wide contacts that do not burn the skin. Secure the harvest in your car, and put a clown mask over their head. The clown mask will disguise the harvest identity from onlookers and prevent the harvest from observing your location.

"Once you secure the harvest, place their car on a flatbed tow truck and cover it up. Ensure you disable the car's electronic devices. If you cannot tow it or disable the electronics, leave the car somewhere prominent, like a nearby parking lot.

"Take the person to a secure location and complete the harvest quickly. Do this in such a way that there is no evidence left behind at the harvest scene. Use an incinerator for any rags contain body fluid, and thoroughly clean all instruments.

"Take the body and his car to a parking lot near a strip club. In the passenger seat of the car, place a newspaper advertisement with the strip club circled. Make sure that the pen used to circle the advertisement is in the car.

"On the harvest's cell phone, text a corrupt politician: 'I will have your money plus drugs by tomorrow morning. This is a one-time payment, and then we're done!' Then text a local drug dealer: 'The meet is on.' Finally, place the phone in the glove box.

"In a secluded area near the car and club, place the body, stab it multiple times with a knife, and pull out some organs. Place chicken feathers and a small voodoo trinket in the open wound. Scatter a sizeable amount of cocaine on the ground.

"Use a propane torch to burn the harvest in the area around the soldering iron burns. Throw the knife and propane torch in the bushes. Place a thousand dollars, a thumb drive with a random-number-generated data file named 'encrypted evidence,' and some low-quality diamonds in the harvest's sock. Do an area check, and then leave by a different route.

"This harvest has to have a good number of plausible red herrings: the strip club, the corrupt politician, the file that cannot be decoded, voodoo, the diamonds, and a botched drug deal. In this example, I have listed an excessive number to illustrate the point. As a guideline, I recommend three."

This wild description amazed me. Grace smiled and said, "Your turn. You uncover a youth counselor who is stealing money and abusing boys."

Wow, I was not expecting this. *How about I call the police and report this person?* No, that will not work. *Alright, I can do this.* I took several creative writing classes, and the perfect murder topic was popular.

I began: "First off, I would get a look at the records of the place to see if the theft is occurring. Then I would talk to the parents of the abused children."

I was rather proud of myself—Detective J.K. on the case. Grace gave me a "you were being an idiot" look and scolded, "Take our time together more seriously. It takes a month or more to identify a harvest and plan. Also, you left the most obvious trail possible for the authorities to follow. Try again."

I realized I should have tried harder. I thought for a while and said in a confident voice, "I would ignore the theft angle, as this is not important."

Grace did not react but appeared to be listening. I continued, "I would enter the youth center posing as a parent wanting to enter my child into their program and ask for a tour. First, I would ask the kids how they like their youth counselor. As you said, look into their eyes. If the children looked like they were hiding something, I would investigate further. I don't read eyes like you do, but I can spot when a child is unhappy.

"Now, I would need an excuse to speak to the potential harvest person. I would tell them a friend knew the person and I would like to speak with them. When this potential harvest came to me, I would say my friend's son didn't like this counselor. There should be a reaction. I would read the reaction and make a determination."

"You would kill a man on that weak evidence?!" Grace snapped at me.

I paused and stammered, "Well . . . I would inquire about their motives with the soldering iron."

I smiled, feeling I had built a tight case. People talk when being burned. I had witnessed that sight twice this week, and I would remember their painful expressions for the rest of my life. Grace was not amused by my performance and said,

"Try harder. You cannot read people yet. This skill took many years to perfect, and even with an infinite amount of time, you might not have the ability in you. Without seeing intent or an actual crime, you should not proceed. I will give you an easy one. A homeless man is walking down the street while striking people."

I thought I had the youth counselor nailed. So I thought for a long moment and said, "I would follow this person and see where they lived."

Grace cut me off. "Homeless people smell bad and are unhealthy. They often have severe mental problems. The correct answer is to pass. You are not grasping the basic concepts.

"Let's try another easy one: A truly evil person is released from prison because of a technicality. What do you do?"

I knew I was on thin ice. My new goal was to keep Grace happy. So I took a long time to think. "Let's look at the bigger picture," I began. "The end game would be to make it look like the youth counselor is the person who committed the murder."

Grace seemed amused, and I filled in the details. "We know people do not like this prisoner, but they are probably good people, so we do not want them to get blamed for the harvest. We also know about the youth counselor. So I would build a motive framework around the prison person, using child porn supplied by the youth counselor."

Grace shook her head and said, "The problem is that you think like a storyteller. Unexpected events occur at the worst possible times. It is not enough to blame another person. The authorities do not always pursue the most obvious suspect. You did not consider the crime scene.

"Do you know how I find my harvest subjects? I developed a commercial service for law enforcement that catalogs unsolved crimes. Often, a person is a suspect in several unsolved crimes. If you watch this suspected person, a pattern will emerge. In addition, the Internet now makes it possible to observe a person without meeting them.

"Often, I know a person is evil far in advance of meeting them. An evil person is not evil in one part of their life. Their evil has a far reach. Even their choices in movies, books, and people they associate with show the same pattern.

"The correct answer is to make sure they are alone and then make a quick grab. Take the body to a nearby field and put a copy of the paper with their release notice near them. If you want to blame the youth counselor, steal his cell phone and leave it near the body."

Grace stopped speaking, and I knew enough not to upset her, so I waited in silence. The minutes ticked by, and I sat patiently. Then, suddenly, I knew I was being watched. I turned, and Heathcliff was staring at me. I thought she had a disappointed look on her mountain lion face. *What was the deal with this place?* I was such an outsider. *How can a mountain lion look disappointed?* I felt like saying, "We should get Heathcliff to yank the bodies out of the house, and then everybody would know what happened."

Heathcliff snorted, and it sounded like a laugh. I looked at Grace, and she smiled wickedly for an instant. Then her upset expression returned. I turned back to Heathcliff and asked in a funny voice, "Not enough Friskies today?"

Heathcliff glanced at me with a "you are an idiot" look. She then stomped her front right paw. The action made little noise, but I felt the movement throughout my body. Heathcliff had sent me a simple message: *You know, it would be fun to rip you in half.*

I got scared, sat up straight, and said in a soft voice, "Sorry, I misspoke."

Grace smiled slightly, and Heathcliff grinned. *How can a mountain lion know what I am saying?* Grace got up, walked into the next room, and returned with several books of different sizes. She sat down and said, "You must rethink your situation. This is not a game or a movie. It is now clear that you do not understand how serious it is to take a life and why you must do this. I was going to spend tomorrow on our next task, but we must advance our schedule. I kept a record of every harvest, and I will discuss each one in great detail. Please write what I say."

Grace took a small, well-worn book and read. It was a description of her first harvest. She included her feelings, mistakes, and possible improvements. I wrote everything in my notebook and did not speak until she stopped reading.

Lunch was bread and cheese. I do not remember the taste. We ate in silence and then left the kitchen without cleaning up. I noticed Grace left crumbs on the floor, which amused me.

We returned, and I continued writing without questions. We broke for dinner, then continued well into the night. Late in the evening, my hand hurt too much to continue. I had recorded all of her harvests up to 1963. My head was spinning with facts; it was too much to process. I said good night, headed for my bathroom, and found a neat pile of tan pajamas near the bathroom door. I still could not figure out how Grace made these neat piles. I washed up, went to the bedroom, and found it empty.

I noticed Heathcliff was not lying on the bed. "Heathcliff," I said in a louder than conversation voice. A head popped around the corner like I had said, "Scooby Snack." I looked at Heathcliff with amusement and said, "Come on. Let's get some sleep, you little bed stealer."

Heathcliff once again grinned and padded right past me into the bed. I got into the bed and looked at her face for a long time. Then, I held my hand up to her paw. It was larger than my hand and had enormous claws that were thicker than my thumb. Heathcliff was looking right at me and seemed content. "You know that Heathcliff is a boy's name?" I asked her.

Heathcliff rolled her head and looked at me with an expression that said, "Yeah, I know." She moved her head from shoulder to shoulder and then shrugged. This gesture surprised me. "Do you understand me?" I asked.

Heathcliff seemed to nod. *Alright, this was getting unreal. I looked at Heathcliff's big yellow eyes and said, "Is there something you want?"

I got a distant image of a bowl of water. *What the heck? Is this even possible? You are a cat— rather, a mountain lion. I am a human, and it does not work that way.* Not knowing what else to do, I got up, and we both walked into the kitchen. I found a mixing bowl and poured water into it. Heathcliff lapped it up and seemed happy. Then went back to the bedroom and climbed into bed. I sensed she was tired, put my arm around her, and that was how my day ended.

TEN

Grace had given me four hundred years of harvesting. As an author, I did not know how to present this vast amount of information. A chronological list of all her harvests would be interesting but repetitive—like reading four hundred years of obituaries. I thought about a timeline or story summary, but those approaches would be confusing blobs. Eventually, I settled on statistics to 1963 with highlights.

1498 to 1963 is 465 years, and in that time, Grace harvested 2,291 people or 4.9 per year. She began with two per year, and by 1963, it was six. This increase agreed with her suggestion that the host body gets used to the process and, later in life, more harvests are required. Of the total, she did not intend to harvest 74 people, but they were recently dead or dying. Most people were injured in wars, fires, or accidents, and she was in the area.

Grace took the lives of 536 people who were not harvested. Of these, 51 were unintentional, 321 threatened her safety, and she did not like the other 164. Of the 51 people she took unintentionally, the majority discovered her harvesting and had to be killed to protect her secret. Accidents in which Grace was involved took fourteen innocent lives, just as car crashes take lives today.

Of the 51 people whose deaths were unintentional, seventeen were children, and most of them had been defending their parents. Grace went into great detail on each one and how bad she felt about taking their life. Each death provided a lesson to better improve her technique. She never repeated her mistakes, and the last child died in 1722.

Of the harvests, 93.2 percent were men. Grace did not record ages, but she said harvesting a person over thirty-five did not yield positive results and under the age of twenty yielded unpredictable results. Twenty-four people escaped before being harvested, and three were recaptured.

A typical harvest entry: "June 11, 1892. Houston, Texas. Harvest: Billy Madison; stagecoach robber. He bragged about killing eleven people. I waited until he made camp and took him from behind. Billy was unremorseful. I buried him and his saddle under a tree. Then I cleaned up the campsite, and set his horse free."

Some had no detail: "May 21, 1711. Ireland. Harvest: angry man."

Others had an abundance of detail: "July 9, 1595. Red house on Bolshaya Belozerskaya Street outside Dmitriyev. Harvest: Efimova Voronin; child abuser. He was in charge of a small school and took great pleasure in abusing the children, especially the older girls. Efimova was a short, balding man of substantial girth. He had no children of his own and a mean-spirited wife who despised him. He had a toxic relationship with the woman next door, and I observed him four days before the harvest.

"Efimova had a regular pattern, and I took him at night on his walk home. I chose the abduction location between two houses, where there was no light. I tripped him, knocked his head into the snow, bound him, and then placed a white cotton gag into his mouth. Efimova put up a struggle as I pulled him into a cart. We rode off into the woods, where I took great pleasure in the harvest. Efimova had no remorse for his despicable actions. He had eleven coins in his left pocket, and I placed these in the local poor box.

"I made the body look like a bear attacked him and left it in the woods. I added a new distraction of fresh bear scat. Efimova had a curious scar on his leg that looked like a heart. The bear-footprint walking shoes worked well.

"This was the third time I used the hot poker stick. I added five seconds between burns. This delay improved the harvesting effect. The mint-oil solution also worked better at twenty-five degrees centigrade. My incision pain was average. Next time, I will try twenty-six centigrade and burn the victim's heel, which is highly sensitive to pain. An idea occurred to me to have a chair with a mirror to help with the stitches."

The following entries stood out:

"June 18, 1526. The road. Harvest: Miska; slave owner. I had been waiting all day for my next harvest. Then, off in the distance, a large triple carriage appeared, pulled by fourteen magnificent horses. The carriages were colorful, with beautiful decorations. There was only one driver, a grand woman dressed in an elegant Damascus green. I had never encountered a woman dressed in fine cloth such as this. She wore two guns and whipped each horse with great precision.

"I suspected there were several people in the carriages, and I knew it would have been foolish to attempt a harvest. I hid in the forest, but the woman observed me from her high carriage position. She stopped the horses, set the brake, and jumped down.

"This large woman moved more quickly than I imagined and soon cornered me near two trees. She grabbed me by my arm and dragged me toward her carriages. As she did so, I pretended to cry. When I sensed she had let her guard down, I used my concealed knife and slashed her left Achilles tendon. The woman fell, then howled curse words and reached for her guns. I was too quick for her and held each arm down with my knees.

"The woman was fierce, putting up a great fight while yelling and spitting at me. Some of her curse words I knew, and some I did not. I slashed her in the neck, and she stopped struggling. I dragged her to a secluded area, completed the harvest, and concealed the body. My plan was to give the horses a slap to make it appear as if the woman had fallen off.

"When I approached the carriages, I heard women's voices. When I opened the first carriage, there was a grand living area. The second carriage contained clothes, supplies, and cooking instruments. The voices were coming from the third, and I opened the door while holding one of her guns.

"Inside, I saw six women locked up in chains. The women spoke in broken Russian and asked what I was going to do with them. I undid their chains, and the prisoners told me that the woman, known as Miska, had taken them as sex slaves. She forced them to go from town to town as a caravan of prostitution, complete with a dancing stage show.

"I gave each girl a horse, food, and a share of the money that I found on the body. I told them I would clean up the carriages, and nobody would ever find Miska. The girls thanked me for their freedom and rode away.

"I took the three carriages and the remaining horses to the same place where Cleo had had her camp. At the bottom of the first carriage, I found a hidden chest, and it was full of coins. The first carriage also contained fantastic artwork and other treasures. This was the beginning of my interest in art.

"Miska was the first woman I harvested. Up to this point, I had not met a woman as evil as a man."

"July 1, 1528. The road. Harvest: unknown man; loathsome person. This man spat in my face and called out a curse as he rode by in his cart. I said nothing to upset this man or known him before. I quickly decided to take him, and I jumped onto his cart, stabbed him in both eyes, and then dragged him to the ground. I harvested him without stunning him and left him to die.

"It was then I noticed a small girl watching me. She looked at me with a sweet, confused expression and asked, 'What are you doing to my daddy?' She had been in the back of his cart under a blanket. I looked at her, and she started to run. I chased after her and brought her down. I did not want to kill her, but she would not stop screaming. I was afraid that some-body else from the road would hear me, and I had no choice but to silence her by force.

"Afterward, the now-still body saddened me deeply. I carried her away and made a proper grave beside the road. I visited that grave for many years. Then, one day, I went to pay my respects, and workers had widened the road. In doing so, they eliminated her grave. I did not know if they moved her gravesite or covered it up. The lesson I learned was always to check carts for hidden children."

"August 5, 1734. Outside Chomutov, Czech Republic. Harvest: unknown man and woman; evil people. This was my first trip away from my home. I learned a man and a woman were going from town to town, taking children, killing them, and eating their flesh.

"At that time, the authorities were not organized enough to recognize criminal patterns. Even if they knew what to look for, they did not have enough men to organize an effective search. It took me three weeks to find and locate the pair. They were wretched people dressed in torn clothing, without hats. I took them to a secluded spot and started the harvest. I considered the idea of placing two pancreases in my shoulder but chose not to.

"I stunned both people and tied them up. Then, while taking out my harvesting equipment, I noticed a hunting party of three boys and a man had unexpectedly come out of the forest. I knew witchcraft was a punishable offense. However, I did not want to kill three boys, so I told them that these two people had killed my children, and I was taking my revenge.

"The pair could still talk and, in their crazy state, confirmed how vile they were. I asked the man not to allow the boys to be a part of my revenge, and they retreated into the forest. After the harvest, I left in a hurry and did not hide the bodies. I have never encountered two people that, together, behaved so abhorrently."

"December 2, 1805. Austerlitz, Austria. Harvest: unknown soldier; murderer. I was traveling through Austria looking for art when war broke out. There was a fierce battle, and the French armies of Marshal of the Empire Louis-Nicolas Davout had won a great victory.

"I watched the battle from a nearby house and came out after the fighting had ceased. Many wounded soldiers confronted me as the able-bodied soldiers had moved on. The medics had not yet arrived to take the wounded away.

"A Russian soldier with a leg wound was using his bayonet to kill injured French soldiers. I walked up to him, slashed his neck, and harvested him in a bomb crater on the battlefield.

"Unknown to me, I was being watched. As I left the battlefield, several soldiers approached me. A decorated soldier got off his horse and kissed both of my cheeks. He thought I was desecrating the body of an enemy soldier. The soldier gave me a war medal, and the men all rode away. They did not ask about the harvest or why I was there. I still have the medal."

"February 22, 1815. Paris, France. Harvest: Jean-Charles Delafosse; murderer. I had been observing this unusual individual for two months. He killed evil people and took their money. I was curious to learn if Jean-Charles was a harvester, as he took great effort to disguise his crime as murder by someone else. Moreover, he often went to elaborate means to place blame on corrupt city officials.

"I collected evidence from several crime scenes before the authorities arrived, so I could expose him as a thief who was killed by one of his victim's family members.

"Jean-Charles lived in a small shed behind a horse stable, and I waited inside. When he arrived, I had no difficulty binding and gagging him. I brought him to a nearby farm.

"Jean-Charles did not scream when I gave him his first hot poke. I asked him if he had anything to say, and he replied, 'I committed many crimes, and I will now answer for my misdeeds. I only ask that you give the small amount of money I have in my possession to the Château de Chaban orphanage.' When I further questioned him, he said he was raised there, and the workers were his only family. France was going through hard economic times, and the orphanage was not receiving donations. I spared his life.

"We spent the afternoon discussing the technical aspects of committing a murder, and we shared techniques. It disappointed me to learn that he was not a harvester. I gave him the evidence I had collected and told him how I discovered his activities. He wanted to know my motivation for taking lives, but I did not reveal the truth. I took him back to his shed and gave him a donation for the orphanage. He was the first person with whom I shared my secrets. I intended to keep in touch with him, but he died eight months later under mysterious circumstances."

"August 15, 1840. Cottontown, South Carolina. As I was traveling through the Southern United States, a white man beat a young slave to death on his work crew for no reason. I followed the man from a discrete distance and found that he worked on a nearby plantation. For a week, I observed him and found that he lived in a bunkhouse with several other men.

"I disguised myself with curly red hair, a blue shirt, and men's pants. I carefully made my way up to the bunkhouse, and I listened outside as they described reprehensible acts. My intent had been to harvest this one individual, but I changed my mind. Entering a nearby supply house, I located several containers of lamp oil and doused the outside of the bunkhouse. Then, with the doors and windows secured, I set the fire. While it burned, I watched, satisfied by the screams. These evil men would never harm another soul.

"The plantation owner confronted me as I was mounting my horse. I shot him in the groin and rode away. My 'curly red hair' description was in the paper the next day, and they called me 'the Red Barnstorm.'"

"January 15, 1888. East London. Harvest: unknown woman; thief and murderer. This was at the height of the Jack the Ripper scare in London. I discovered a woman posing as a prostitute was robbing men, killing them, and dumping their bodies into the sewer. I observed her for a week, and she killed three men.

"This woman had an icy heart, and it was easy to seduce her with the promise of money. I used an empty house that I told her was full of rich men and harvested her in the kitchen. I dressed up the cuts like the description in the newspaper and made the crime scene look like Jack the Ripper had been responsible for the death. Her death was in every newspaper, and they listed her as his ninth victim. I do not know if there was a real Jack the Ripper, and I suspect the authorities incorrectly linked separate crimes to one fictional person."

"January 15, 1905. Köln, Germany. Harvest: Dietz Schreiber; murderer. I had been attempting to locate this man for six months. Dietz would kill or hurt people for no reason, then disappear. The authorities suspected they had a multiple murderer in their midst.

"I caught up to Dietz in a market while he was attempting to seduce a young woman. When our eyes met, the sight shocked me. This man had no energy, as though he were devoid of a soul. Nevertheless, he did not resist capture, and I took him to a nearby abandoned building.

"After I secured Dietz, he pleasantly gave his name and said he understood why he was being punished. When I asked him why he was killing people, he said he was doing the work of the devil. I applied the hot poker stick, and while Dietz moved in pain, he did not scream.

"Right before I harvested Dietz, he informed me that hunting down evil people was an important service. He encouraged me to keep up my righteous efforts and never stop.

"The effects lasted a full year. I suspect he was so evil that his pancreas put up a tremendous fight, which prolonged the harvest effect. I did some wonderful paintings and poems during that period. I have never met somebody so devoid of life. Dietz promised he would return in a different form, but our paths have never crossed."

"August 11, 1936. Gladewater, Texas. Harvest: James McCaw; rapist. I was on my way back from my latest investment. I had purchased 10,000 acres near Gladewater.

Beforehand, I had consulted a geologist who confirmed the land contained oil. I had drilled fifty-one oil wells, and almost all of them produced.

"As the profit was dramatic, I went to Gladewater to see the operation for myself. After the site visit, I drove my Chevrolet Baby Grand on a remote dirt road when six men on horses stopped me. The lead man said, 'Stop in the name of the law. We are the Texas Rangers. My name is Deputy James McCaw, and you are under arrest, little lady.' They smiled big with their hands on their revolvers, but they had not taken them out of their holsters. I asked about my crime, and they all laughed. James said, 'Now how about you take your clothes off, then we can discuss your *crime*.'

"The men were foolish to think I would surrender. So I slid into the passenger seat and retrieved two 1911 Browning pistols. I shot the first man in his left eye and the second man in the forehead.

"James was on my left, and there were three men behind me. I spun to my right and shot the next man in the heart, the next through the nose, and the last through his mouth. I continued twisting until I had both guns pointed at James. I was happy with my display of marksmanship and motioned to him. His revolver was still in his holster, and he looked at me with his mouth open. James exclaimed, 'You just shot four men!' It was five. He started to pull out his revolver, and I shot him in the heart."

"August 10, 1955. Valdai, Russia. Harvest: unknown crazy woman. I was visiting the land that had once been my family home while enjoying an apple from our tree. A disheveled woman emerged from the forest and approached. She had black, grimy hair, dirty clothes, and gnarly teeth. She started spinning, praying, and accusing me of being the source of all evil.

"I tried to calm her down, but she produced a rusty knife and tried to cut me. I disarmed her and continued my attempt to pacify her. She said a woman had been haunting this forest for four hundred years, and I was that person. She claimed that the ghosts in the area had told her this. One of them was a little girl who died after I had stabbed her father's eyes out.

"I made every attempt to explain that I was passing through. However, the woman did not accept my explanation and continued her verbal and physical assault. Finally, I had no choice but to harvest her. I placed the body in a remote area covered by a large tree.

"This harvest brought up many memories; in particular, the memory of taking the young girl. Valdai had become a much larger town since I was young. I made inquiries about the woman, and she was locally known as 'the crazy one.' Her insight into my past was unsettling, and I never understand the source."

The morning after Grace described her harvests, I was having a dream about Heathcliff. She was a young kitten, playing with her mountain lion mother and Grace. I began understanding how they met: Heathcliff's mother was Grace's pet mountain lion. It was a strange and distant memory filled with curiosity and wonder.

I knew something was hitting my face. I opened my eyes to find Heathcliff staring at me. She had been using her right paw to nudge me awake. The pads of Heathcliff's feet felt rough and uneven. Her expression was strange—perhaps painful or cold.

Heathcliff placed her paw on my chest and brought her face close to mine. Our eyes played a crazy game, and I got a strange thirdhand image in my mind. It was taken when I had harvested the man known as Richard. The sight frightened me, and I realized Heathcliff had been watching my harvest. I looked into Heathcliff's eyes and got a strong feeling of satisfaction and warmth.

Heathcliff sent me another moving image: of Grace asleep next to me. I visualized her arm tightly around me and a satisfied expression on her face. Grace was breathing softly, and so was I. During that moment, I knew she was truly happy for the first time in a long while. A feeling of comfort and warmth from Heathcliff accompanied the image. I then got a sensation that she needed something from me. I did not understand what it was, and we looked at each other for a long moment. It occurred to me that a critical part of Heathcliff's life was missing, and the only answer I came up with was that she regretted not having offspring. I felt a deep sense of connection to this fantastic creature. Heathcliff looked at me, showed her big teeth in what seemed like a smile, got up, and walked toward the door. She looked at me again for a long moment, then left. I did not know what it all meant or how she placed moving images into my mind.

I got up, stretched, and noticed a small, neat pile of clothes. I opened the packet, and it was not what I was expecting. The clothing was made out of thick green cloth, and the design was plumber meets businessman-on-a-hunting trip. I put them on and walked into the kitchen.

Grace was holding a plate and eating a small breakfast. Heathcliff was eating what appeared to be coarse ground beef from a plate. Grace motioned to a plate that had eggs, toast, and ham. I found this strange, as we were eating in the kitchen, which seemed forbidden in the past.

I had been expecting another long day of recording her life from 1963 to the present and then asking questions. "Heathcliff wanted to spend some time with you," Grace said. "You may use the boots near the door, and I have prepared a lunch."

"I do not understand," I lightly protested. "I thought I was going to get more details from you."

Grace looked at me and then walked away. I looked down at Heathcliff, and she seemed to be patiently waiting for me to finish. I ate breakfast, washed my plate, then inspected my eating area for crumbs. As I did so, I was sure that Heathcliff was laughing.

I put on a pair of boots and found a small backpack Grace had left for me. Heathcliff seemed happy and bounded off toward the woods. I watched her run off and wondered what I should do. I could not run as fast as Heathcliff, so I walked in her general direction.

The woods in Oregon are dense, with many exposed roots, so I moved with great caution. There was no visible trail where Heathcliff had entered. My progress was slow, and I tripped many times. Every so often, I would come across Heathcliff as she waited triumphantly for me. Sometimes she walked beside me, and as she did so, she would occasionally look up at me. I could tell that she liked being with me and was enjoying her surroundings.

I realized I completely depended on Heathcliff as a guide. I did not even have a compass.

At one point, she walked beside me, and I felt her impending excitement. She started bounding rather than walking. We soon came to a clearing, and she guided me to the left side, where she played with a stick. This stick had many deep teeth marks and was chewed off at the ends. I watched with quiet fascination as she expertly maneuvered it in her mouth.

It suddenly dawned on me she had been here many times before. As she gnawed, she occasionally looked at me with what could be called a smile. I did not know whether or not I should play with her. A part of me wanted to playfully grab at the stick or throw it, so she could bring it back. However, I got the distinct impression my interference would not be well-received.

Heathcliff dropped the stick, and we circled to reach the other side of the clearing. She darted up a small rock outcrop with ease. Heathcliff climbed into an indentation that allowed her head to be visible, and she took a long moment to observe the environment with great intensity. From this vantage point, she had an excellent view of me and the surrounding area. I could see the indentation was carefully chosen, as it concealed her from casual observation.

I looked into her eyes for a long moment and, slowly, I understood. This was *her* home, this was *her* rock, and this was *her* world. She had invited a guest into her special place. I looked into her eyes and asked, "Have you taken Grace here?"

Heathcliff intensified her stare, but I did not get a mental impression. Soon, she seemed content, and she relaxed. I watched her tail playfully flip up a four times. I had never observed her acting so casually. Finally, with nothing else to do, I found a rock to sit on. I wanted to eat lunch, but this did not seem to be the right time.

Instead, I opened myself up to the process and relaxed in what little sun there was. I looked at the woods and smelled the air while watching the clouds go by. A long while later, Heathcliff got up and then quickly disappeared. I did not think she wanted me to follow. So I continued to enjoy the sun, and then I walked around the clearing while pondering the day's events.

Several minutes later, Heathcliff reappeared with a bird in her mouth. I followed her to a different rock, and she began eating. This sight was graphic, but I understood this was how she ate. I also understood it was now lunchtime, and I opened up the backpack. Grace packed a roast beef sandwich, a slice of blueberry pie, and a mason jar full of juice. She included nothing for Heathcliff.

Lunch was, of course, outstanding, and afterward, we walked back to the rock, where Heathcliff once again took up her intense observation of the surrounding area. Occasionally, I caught Heathcliff glancing at me.

After a while, it occurred to me I had the wrong perception of Heathcliff. Initially, I treated her like a wild animal. Then, after we had a connection, I treated her as a person. This was because of her ability to interact with me at a high level. It dawned on me that this outlook was utterly wrong.

She was an *adult* mountain lion, and I was now in *her* world. I realized the point of our trip into the woods was for me to better understand her. I looked at Heathcliff, and she nodded in my direction. I did not comprehend how she knew I had made a breakthrough in understanding our relationship.

An hour later, the sun was setting, and we started walking back. I ran into many branches and tripped over countless roots. Heathcliff walked with grace and purpose, without a single misstep. However, I noticed her pace was slower, and her steps no longer bounced.

I was glad to see the lights of Grace's house when we arrived late in the evening. I met her at the door, and she motioned for me to take off my boots. We had a light dinner of noodles in a meat sauce, which tasted fantastic. Unfortunately, Grace was not in the mood for conversation. I sensed something heavy was on her mind, and I hoped I had not unknowingly messed up again.

Afterward, I took a shower, and an enormous amount of mud washed off. I then went into my bedroom, where Heathcliff was already asleep. As I slipped under the covers, her eyes opened briefly. I could tell she was tired but happy to see me. I smiled, closed my eyes, and placed my hand on her paw. I soon got a warm image of contentment from Heathcliff.

I had almost fallen asleep when Grace asked, "Did you have a pleasant afternoon?"

I looked up in the dim oil light and noticed Grace sitting on the corner of my bed. She was wearing the same nightgown as in our previous encounter. "Yes. Heathcliff took me to her home," I answered in a sleepy voice.

"That is nice to hear. I am glad that you two have a connection."

"Did she ever take you there?" I wanted to know.

"You have a long day ahead of you. Get a good night's rest."

Grace got up and left the room. I wondered what my long day would entail. I turned to look at Heathcliff, and I could tell that she was awake, but her eyes were closed. "Did you have a good day with me?" I wanted to know.

I got the impression she did, though it disappointed me that she did not send me a mental image. Exhausted, I soon fell asleep. That night, I had a dream about our adventure into the woods.

The following day, I woke up and was surprised that Heathcliff was not in bed. I got up with a smile as I had gotten a good night's sleep. As usual, there was a neat pile of clothing in the corner. This time, it was smart blue pants with a lightly striped white shirt. This was by far the best outfit yet, and I felt like a million bucks.

Grace was in the kitchen, and she did not look happy. This sight disappointed me, as I thought we were doing really well. I hoped I had not upset her.

We had a breakfast of coffee, fruit, and pastries. It may have been simple, but of course, the taste was beyond description. I tried to make small talk, but Grace had no interest. We went outside, sat on the porch, and enjoyed the morning air. It felt nice, and we sat next to each other. I thought I should do something, but I could not figure out what that something was.

I had planned to ask Grace how she had improved the harvest technique, but I decided this was not the right time to jump into a line of questions. Heathcliff joined us, and the three of us stared at the trees and the sky. We had been there for half an hour, and I was giving Heathcliff a neck rub when there was a loud bang from behind me.

Heathcliff's head exploded. I was shocked and started screaming. I turned to see Grace holding a handgun. She looked, sad and I pleaded for my life. Finally, Grace put the gun down and looked away.

A short time later, we walked to the barn. Grace got a wheelbarrow and a shovel. I was still crying as we walked back to the now-dead Heathcliff. I had not noticed before, but next to the chair was a nicely folded piece of black cloth. We wrapped Heathcliff up in the fabric and set her gently in the wheelbarrow.

I rolled Heathcliff to a spot inside the forest. Grace directed me to dig and then walked away. I suspected this spot held some significance but did not ask. After I had finished the digging, I gently placed Heathcliff in the hole and covered her up. I then lined the gravesite with stones as a sign of respect.

As I stood while reflecting, I realized Grace was beside me. She held a grave marker in one hand and a bouquet in the other. For once, I was smart enough not to talk. Grace laid the flowers on the grave, and then I put the marker at the head. It was a well-crafted wooden stick that read "Heathcliff."

Grace turned to me and cried on my shoulder for a long time. I held her as we both sobbed uncontrollably. While I had only known Heathcliff for three days, losing a close friend devastated me.

We walked back to the house in tears. In between sobs, Grace murmured that she had been sick for over a year. She said Heathcliff had known it was her time and was glad to meet me. Grace said other words, but I could not understand them. I cried and cried.

We passed by the porch, and she had cleaned away all traces of the incident. We then went into the living room and sat. Unfortunately, Grace firmly informed me it was time for me to leave. I pleaded that I did not have enough information to write a book and asked if I could improve the situation. She firmly said we had spoken enough, and the subject was closed.

Grace gave me a nice leather suitcase filled with the clothes I'd worn the last few days and the clothes I had on at the book signing. She also gave me a tool kit consisting of harvest knives, a one-liter glass container of mint oil, and a travel container with two snakes. There was also was a high-quality color photograph of the scroll that Cleopatra had given her and a neatly typed translation of the scroll.

We loaded my car on the tow truck and covered it with a tarp. I sat in the front seat, and Grace gave me a hood. She reclined the seat so that I would not be noticeable to the other drivers. I felt sad, and riding in the tow truck brought back conflicting memories. My initial assumption that Grace wanted to kill me now seemed absurd.

I still had questions on the drive *somewhere*, but I knew I had to be careful about where I took the conversation. "I think I know why you wanted me to write your story," I started out. "You wanted to determine if there are others like you out there. You want the world to know about the amazing young girl from Russia. The girl who made the world a better place, one evil person at a time."

Grace did not respond, but I knew I was correct and continued, "But how'll the other immortals, or harvesters, or whatever know where to find you?"

Once again, Grace declined to say anything, but somehow, I put it together in my mind and answered my question. "The others will find the apple tree, and then they will find you. It may take a hundred years, but harvesters have all the time in the world."

I think Grace made an "mmm" sound that probably meant yes. I was excited at understanding the great mystery of why Grace kidnapped me. Finally, I felt better and sat back in my seat, knowing all my logic meant something.

Then I had a revelation: "But this won't work. If my book about you is popular, many people will read it, and Russians will translate it. Then people will find your tree. They could use old maps and the Internet. This tree will become a popular destination. People love to have a connection with the past, and you will become a big hero of Russia, even if they never meet you."

Grace had obviously not thought of this angle, and she asked me, "Do you think people would really do this? I cannot imagine they would care."

I hooted and said, "Can't imagine? People love a connection and love to be near famous areas. Look at the Battle of Gettysburg. Thousands of people go there every year to see a bunch of dirt.

"Your living apple tree represents a five-hundred-year journey of a proud Russian girl. They'll probably have a theme park with candy apples from that tree." I laughed and continued, "They'll probably call it Grace-Land."

I found this comical name funny, and I started laughing really hard at my pun. Then, I noticed that Grace was not laughing. Instead, she said quietly, "Those people who harvest will have to find you instead. I will also keep close tabs on you."

That statement took the fun away, and we continued to drive. I wanted to learn more and attempted to get the conversation back on track. "I'm not sure I've gathered enough information to write a complete book. There is still a lot I don't know about your motivation."

Grace said nothing, and I suggested, "Well, you should at least approve the book before it's released."

Grace did not speak, and during the silence, I thought about my Heathcliff dream. I still did not comprehend my connection to this staggering animal. *Had Heathcliff been manipulating my mind? Did I somehow dream about her because I had gone to sleep thinking about her? Had I really been dreaming? Why did Heathcliff take me to her special spot? How did she send me movies? How did she send vivid emotion?*

Typically, I never remember my dreams; they are a jumble of images. However, the more I thought about my memory, the more this dream seemed important. Finally, I put the dream together in my head: a young mountain lion kitten playing with her mother. Grace was there, too, and I felt this scene took place a long time ago.

Then I started making connections—this entire thing: me being here, writing a book, Grace, and Heathcliff. I knew that neither one of them could have children. I began to understand that my recent experiences had nothing to do with a book. They had to do with having a child, and I was the nearest childlike thing that Grace could have. Heathcliff was Grace's best friend, and it was very important to Grace that Heathcliff approves of me. However, I knew something important was missing.

"Heathcliff lived longer than a normal mountain lion!" I blurted out.

There was silence from Grace, and I said, "Like you, Heathcliff couldn't have children. It was really important for Heathcliff to have a child—I mean a kitten. Heathcliff wanted you to meet me and teach me to harvest. You did this whole thing all for her before she died."

There was complete silence from Grace, but I persisted. "There is a lot you haven't told me. I think you withheld the most important part of your story."

We rode in silence for a while, but eventually, Grace spoke up. "Some mysteries should remain mysteries."

"I don't understand. What aren't you telling me? What am I missing?"

I was sure I was correct. However, to my great disappointment, Grace did not reply. A moment later, I sensed we were getting close to our destination. I wanted some closure to this entire experience and asked, "Well, did I live up to your expectations?"

A long moment later, Grace let out a long breath and answered, "I understood you were a poor author when I selected you. However, I was not prepared for the impact of this decision. I must admit it was difficult to interact with you, which was as much my fault as yours. That being said, James, you have exceeded my expectations. In time, you will achieve your goal and become a profound author."

I did not know how to respond to this answer. However, I was happy Grace liked me. "Do you think I lived up to Heathcliff's expectations?" I wondered.

"That is the third time you surprised me. Of course, you did. Heathcliff abhorred the other author and, in general, disliked people. I can honestly say that her last moments with you were her happiest."

I did not know I had had such an effect on Heathcliff. The tow truck came to a stop, and I took my hood off. We were at a remote crossroads, and I watched as Grace let down my car from the tow truck. We looked at each other for a long, silent moment, and I felt lost.

"Well, now what?" I had to ask.

"Write your book. It will be well-received because you will write it from your heart."

I choked up and asked, "When will I see you again?"

Grace smiled but did not reply. It was hard, but I sobbed, "I guess this is goodbye."

Grace gave me a hug and walked toward her tow truck. "I care about you," I whispered.

Grace stopped and whispered without turning around, "Likewise."

I knew she was sad, and the moment was difficult. But, I wanted to say so much more and find out the true story of Heathcliff. "Why will you not tell me about Heathcliff and why I am really here?" I needed to know.

Grace stopped walking and looked at the ground. I knew she applied great effort to hold back her emotions. I walked over to her and put my arm around her shoulder.

Eventually, Grace turned and looked at me. I could see streaks of tears running down her cheeks. She smiled weakly. "At the beginning, my motivation was to share my story. Right now . . . I am not entirely sure."

Grace then took a deep breath and steadied herself. She got in the tow truck and started the engine. Grace took a deep breath and said in a forced, pleasant voice, "I'm going to drive and then stop. When I do, I will deposit your car keys. Do not follow. If you do, there will be consequences. You will find a map and your charged cell phone in your car. Also, I watched the movie *Highlander*, and I now understand why you made the connection to your situation. Not a great plot. However, there was one reward, Christopher Lambert has a nice butt."

"So, you are into cute butts?" I said, teasing.

Grace smiled warmly, and I could still see the tear streaks on her face. She looked away, then back, and drove away. As promised, she stopped about a half-mile away, got out near a fence post, and then continued driving. I took slow steps toward the post, found my keys, and walked back to my car.

ELEVEN

got in my car, started it up, and looked at the four directions I could drive. There was a circle on a map marking my location: I was near Troy, Oregon. I studied the map and tried to figure out where I had been.

I then considered what had happened to me. Before all this, I was an average small-time author working at Best Buy. Then I got captured and forced to experience ten lifetimes worth of emotions in a few days. It was all beyond overwhelming. *Now what?* I did not know. I sat for a while and tried to get a single consistent thought in my head.

With no other ideas, I got out my cell phone and turned it on. I looked at the date; I was gone for eight days. There were over a hundred missed calls, texts, and emails. From my text history, I saw Grace had texted my friends and family: "I will be away for a week to write my next book." She had also texted my manager at Best Buy, stating that there was a death in the family, and I had to go to a funeral. However, the texts did not answer my immediate question: What should I do now?

Reality suddenly hit me. I had witnessed a man being tortured to death. I had tortured an innocent man and taken his life. Grace captured that moment on video and this evidence could convict me. This thought was startling, and suddenly I returned to reality. I knew I could go to prison for the rest of my life. While I was no longer being held against my will, I felt trapped.

I realized there was nothing I could do at the crossroads. So I checked my map and started driving home. When I reached the town of Troy, my phone map directed me to the nearest police office. I did not get out of the car; instead, I stared intently at the word "police."

I had a decision to make, but crazy thoughts clouded my thinking process. I kept going over the pros and cons of turning myself in. The voice in my head had a lot of opinions, but none helped. Finally, a deputy walked by and tapped on my window to ask if he could help.

"No, thank you," I replied.

"Well, if you change your mind, I'll be inside."

I realized I had proof that the crime was not my fault: my strange clothes, the mint oil, the snakes, the Cleopatra scroll. It was all there and was enough to explain something. *My body forced me to murder!* They had to believe me.

I eventually decided to tell the police everything. I reached for the door handle of my car, but the little voice in my head screamed to wait and think some more. I thought of Heathcliff staring at me. That powerful image stayed with me. It was so confusing. *What did a mountain lion have to do with my life? What did her stare mean? Why was she so important? Why did she take me and only me to her spot? Why did she send me those movies with powerful emotions?*

I started the car and drove away. In retrospect, there was no logic behind my decision and, while I was driving, I wondered about my true motives. I knew I was a criminal; I had taken a life and not confessed to the deputy. However, making that decision made me feel better. I was now free of something, but I did not know what that something was.

During my drive, I had a lot of time to think. My main thought was Heathcliff and her significance in what I had experienced. *Should I get a mountain lion? Can I do a mental mind-read of a mountain lion or only Heathcliff? Did I really do a mind-read? Where do you buy a mountain lion, and how much do they cost? Why did I think about a mountain lion? Was this like the Stockholm syndrome, where the captors identify with the criminals, but I identified with a mountain lion?* As I drove, I got even more confused.

Eventually, though, my negative attitude began to change, and I felt good. *I have five hundred years ahead of me!* I thought about the image Heathcliff sent with Grace and me sleeping together. She looked so happy, and this convinced me I was on the right path.

When I arrived home, I jumped out of my car. I was excited; this was the first day of the rest of my life. I did not have plans, but I somehow knew what I was going to do.

My presence surprised my roommates. They had endless questions, and I told them I was writing a book and now had lots of material. Their fundamental questions concerned me dressing like a Victorian-rock-music-video-businessman. I looked at them and smiled. They said I had changed and was a completely different person. I took this as a compliment.

Home felt good, but I needed to get out and see people. The following day, I went into Best Buy and spoke with my manager. He asked about the death in my family and was genuinely concerned. I thanked him for his concern and explained I had lied

I also confessed to inventing the broken-appliance scam. While I would never repeat my mistakes, I acknowledged I had broken his trust and therefore could not continue working. I thanked him for all his help and encouragement.

Later that day, my former manager called a meeting and explained that the broken-appliance scam would not occur again. He asked several workers to take unpaid leave. This upset my Best Buy friends, and many drifted out of my life. I do not blame them for their decision, but I had changed into a more responsible person.

After visiting Best Buy, I drove to the *Portland Tribune* and walked into my former boss's office with a big grin. Unfortunately, he did not remember me and silently motioned toward the door.

I showed him a story I had written about a local election controversy. He liked it and gave me a job. My specialty was locating and interviewing charismatic people. I would give them the basic facts about a local or national issue and ask their opinions. Musicians, homeless people, artists, small-business owners, and city workers all had fantastic life stories and remarkable insight into the issues of the day. The articles wrote themselves, and newspaper sales increased. My writing career was finally off to an honest start.

I worked hard to make peace with Heather and her family. I had to do this separately, as they were not on speaking terms. I offered to help mend fences and pay some of their legal costs. Heather's father was a proud man and told me he would handle their issues without my help. I remain distant friends with Heather's family, and I help them out when they let me.

In our reconciliation, Heather confessed she had not had sex with Jake. She said she had lied out of spite, and I thanked her for her honesty. I later learned that Heather declared bankruptcy and moved to New Mexico to live with a guy she had met online. We have not spoken since. I still care about Heather, and she will always have a place in my heart. But I understand some mistakes cannot be forgiven or corrected.

My publisher Bethany was not pleased when I told her the truth about my *Grime* books. I arranged for all my future *Grime* proceeds to go toward Jack Dunkin's family. They republished *An Oxford Tale of Mischief* without my edits under the original title. I found it amusing that this change brought low sales and used copies of the original *Grime* series [now out of print] went up in price. Another amusing aspect of this publication was that the critics hated *An Oxford Tale of Mischief.* I thought it was a rather good read.

My actions upset Jack Dunkin's family, and they never thanked me for my altruistic act. Had they forgotten how happy they were when I paid them five dollars for their box of "worthless paper?"

After coming clean to the world about my book, I felt a great sense of relief. I wrote a note on my Facebook page explaining what I had done, and many of my *Grime* fans wrote unpleasant responses. But, strangely, only three people unfriended me out of my 1,500 Facebook friends. In two weeks, the unpleasantness blew over, and new fans of the *Grime* series joined me as friends. The public's short attention span astounded me.

With the now steady income I made from the newspaper, I put a down payment on a four-unit apartment building. It was surprising how easy the bank made this process. Taking a hint from Grace, I made this purchase under the auspices of a corporation that did not have my name associated with it.

My roommates and I did a lot of work on the apartment building during weekends. Soon, the place looked great, and I had four paying tenants. Two months later, I purchased another apartment building and then another.

It is surprising, but the further in debt, the more money banks want to lend you. I got a letter today from a bank I had never done business with before offering a $5 million line of credit. Of course, it was at a terrible interest rate, but it was amazing because, four months before, I was down to twenty bucks.

In my spare time, I learned how to play the piano and cook. I surprised myself by being good at both. I never knew I had creative talent beyond writing.

I firmly decided to write a book about this experience. The commitment that I made to Grace to reveal her story was my primary motivation. Another part was to prevent the video of my reprehensible act from surfacing. If Grace keeps her promise, that video of me will never surface. She seems like the kind of woman who keeps a promise. I'm talking to *you*, Grace!

I spent two days organizing my notes to write this book—what to include and, more importantly, what to exclude. This was the first major nonfiction work I had ever written. Eventually, I went with a first-person approach and focused more on myself rather than Grace. I understand this is not how an interview/biography works. However, if Grace had wanted a professionally written biography of her life, she could have hired such an individual and not harvested them! Her unique story required the personal touch of somebody who directly understood the subject. It also gave me a lot of time to think about myself.

I was surprised that Bethany was willing to speak to me after my confession. I gave her 20 pages and an outline of the book you are reading now. She was eager to see the final product, which was a good sign.

My time at the paper allowed me to think about crime, murder, and how to cover up a crime. Unfortunately, Grace was right: I was not ready. My attempts to describe the "perfect crime" were the work of a clumsy amateur.

I found a great resource in the newspaper database. It listed thousands of detailed descriptions of every conceivable way a murder could be orchestrated. I also searched for murder patterns that looked like harvest victims. I found three unsolved crimes that closely fit the harvest pattern. I wondered if Grace's computer skills had uncovered these "unsolved crimes."

I used the newspaper database to search for potential harvest subjects. Reporters loaded the database with facts, history, notes, and suspicions on every single immoral person in the world. This gave me an excellent understanding of the very worst people our society produced.

I used my newspaper connections to work with the city coroner while writing an article about pancreatic cancer. In exchange for some cleanup help, she allowed me as much time as I wanted to dig around the human body (under her supervision, of course.) As a result, I now am much better informed about how to execute a harvest. In addition, my *new* technique of cutting through the back to quickly gain access to the pancreas impressed her, and she is writing a paper on the topic.

I began taking martial arts classes and going to the gun range. I did not like being helpless or easily captured. These new skills provided more self-confidence, and I have improved my physical strength.

I studied the Cleopatra scroll for many hours. Grace's translation was excellent, and the exquisite anatomical drawings and detailed descriptions blew me away. However, the scroll harvest description was different from the one that Grace performed. Cleopatra used finely ground-up mint paste instead of mint oil. She also placed the pancreas in the left shoulder and used wale oil instead of kidney extract. I do not know why Grace changed the process.

Another part of Cleopatra's scroll attempted to describe how the procedure worked. It explained, "The body is a rope that must be held together. In time, blood breaks the body rope. This sun gift [this is what Cleopatra called the harvest] uplifts the blood and restores the rope to the life of a child." I found it fascinating that before modern laboratory equipment, Cleopatra understood how this procedure works.

I have thought about why Grace chose me to capture her story. She told me I was her second choice, as the first author had been a disappointing failure. It puzzled me why she would seek

an admittedly miserable person like myself. I began to understand she was seeking out a person who desperately needed to
understand himself in order to understand her. I became a blank
canvas on which she could paint her story. This placed me in the
perfect position to absorb what I was writing about.

However, I suspected there was more to it. So I researched
Jack Dunkin in the newspaper database and found out that
he had used a pen name: Edmund Summers. Edmund wrote
several acclaimed books. Apparently, his family was unaware;
otherwise, they would not have sold his papers.

I also found out that Jack Dunkin had an English degree from
Georgetown University. I traced his scholarship to the Morrison
Shipping Company. I suspect Grace knew Jack or provided his
scholarship. I now feel my selection may have been a personal
choice, as I had dishonored her friend.

I used the newspaper database to look for two missing people
who matched the description of the harvested men. Specifically,
I searched for a missing tabloid writer. Despite hours of work, I
came up blank, and I suspect the crime was so well covered up
it raised no suspicions. It is likely the men might not have been
reported missing.

I also used the newspaper database and the Internet to look
up the names of people Grace had harvested before 1963. I
found several crimes going back to 1850 that matched Grace's
accounts. Of note, I found Deputy James McCaw and five other
Texas Rangers were shot outside of Gladewater, Texas. This was
a chilling discovery.

I spent an entire day looking at farms and houses on Google
Maps. Eventually (and amazingly), I was abducted outside

Greenhorn, Oregon. It was a vast property with a single dwelling, and it was for sale. The seller was a faceless East Coast logistics corporation. The real estate agent said the corporation used the property as a retreat, and I arranged a sales visit.

The long drive brought back memories of Grace, and the apple trees looked as wonderful as I remembered. The lawn still did not have a single weed, and the air smelled fresh. While walking around, I found the kitchen still smelled like baked bread.

Inside, everything had been removed, which made the house feel cold. When I went into the rooms, their small size surprised me. The doors I had dared not open were closets. There was a small office and a home entertainment room. The size did not connect with the vast amount of money Grace apparently had.

I walked to the harvest site, and all traces were gone. In its place were newly planted trees. The only reminder of Grace was Heathcliff's grave. I was surprised to see a well-used copy of *Grime: At the End* leaning against the grave marker. To the dismay of the real estate agent, I picked flowers and placed them on the gravesite.

When I did not make an offer, the real estate agent was disappointed, but the asking price was $35 million because of the massive lot size. I whimsically considered purchasing it, but it was far beyond what I could afford. A week later, the real estate agent emailed me that the property was purchased by a large corporation. I suspect that Grace may have been behind this purchase.

I looked into the corporate records for shipping, accounting, and Texas oil wells to find a common link. However, the more I looked into faceless corporations, the less I found. I also researched companies that bought or sold compact discs without success.

I discovered a 1,500-piece art auction that had recently occurred in France. I recognized one painting from Grace's house. I suspect this painting was a personal message from Grace to me: *What happened, really happened!*

The art in the auction came from several corporate collections. The auction house said that "every piece was an undiscovered masterpiece with superb provenance that represented the very best work by the respective artist." This auction was the largest sale of artwork in recent history and generated nearly half a billion dollars. The auction house promised there would be four additional auctions.

I spent a lot of time unraveling why Grace wanted me to tell her story to the world. She promised to reveal the actual reasons behind my abduction when we parted company, but her answers were vague and incomplete.

The first part of the answer may lie in why Cleopatra passed along her secrets to Grace. This amazing young Russian girl fascinated Cleopatra, and she saw something of herself in Grace. This choice may have left an impression on Grace, and she wanted to do the same. I am not sure how I fit the bill of an idealistic young Russian girl, but that is the best explanation I can offer.

The second part is that Grace is a private person. She had no close friends except Heathcliff. I believe she needed someone to confide her secrets to. In time, this person might become a friend she could trust. Therefore, it was important that her best friend—Heathcliff—approve of this choice.

Every night, I go to sleep thinking about Heathcliff. This cat was a complete mystery. She was an amazingly dangerous animal—possibly telepathic—who potentially lived well beyond her average lifespan. I did a lot of research on feline anatomy. It differs vastly from human anatomy, and the pancreas-harvest procedure would not work. Also, Heathcliff had short hair, and I did not see any scars. This left me with an enigma: Did Heathcliff really live longer than normal?

The dreams, telepathic moves, and Heathcliff being able to understand my words are unfathomable. Cats and humans are different species with completely different brain structures. Yet, somehow, we could communicate.

My biggest question is: Why was bringing me to her *home* so important? My only answer is it was her dying wish to share the significance of this sacred location with somebody she cared about. As Heathcliff could not share this fantastic gift with her kitten, she bestowed this honor upon me. However, it made me wonder why she did not bring Grace along on her last adventure.

The close relationship between Heathcliff and Grace is also an enigma. It appears to have spanned many years and perhaps many generations. This was what I thought about the most. After all my thinking and research, I am no closer to understanding Heathcliff. When Grace said, "Some mysteries should remain mysteries," I did not recognize the great truth in that statement.

The person known as Grace, Anitchka Ermolaev, or Barbara Edwards remains a complete mystery. I did an extensive search and came up with nothing. While I keep looking for Grace, our paths have not crossed. Yet, in my heart, I know she will always be close to me.

EPILOGUE

Six months after our encounter, my body slowed down. I knew I had a decision to make: I could go back to my old life with no consequences, or I could live like a king forever. From the perspective of the reader, it may not seem like a tough choice. The obvious answer is to live forever as a wealthy king.

I would become a vigilante antihero who would take care of predators the authorities could not touch. As for the murder, I could outsource it. The Internet or "dark web" makes this anonymous, easy and affordable.

However, talking whimsically about murder and actually committing murder are unrelated concepts. I used my own hands to stop a beating heart in a living human being. That is *by far* what shames me the most. I think about that moment every hour of every day. Those men did not deserve torture or death, no matter their crime. The result was pure, selfish, personal gain. Yet, it was the right thing to do. Nobody else was standing up for their victims or the people that they would hurt in the future.

For me, it is still a choice: kill or let nature kill me. *What did I decide?* Well, will not tell you. Cops read books, too. In fifty years, you will either read a sequel or not. Life has to have some mystery to it.

–James Kimble 10/8/2012

PS. Eventually, I read the book *The Mosquito Coast* by Paul Theroux. It did not technically explain how a propane refrigerator works, but it was a good read.

PSS. No, I did not get a mountain lion, but I want one:)

ABOUT THE AUTHOR

This story evolved from several stories I thought about for many years. However, while I was writing it, I ran into a big problem: I wanted several chapters of Grace's harvest experiences, but, like I stated in the book, it read like a bunch of obituaries, and I restructured the plot.

The character of James is an author like me, but our personalities and lives are unrelated. I have never worked at Best Buy, but I worked at Kinko's for a year. Wow, a murder story based on my Kinko's experiences would be depressing and too close to home.

I liked the character of Grace. She was a strong woman who turned an awful situation to her advantage. So it was essential to make the character female. If I made her male, the only realistic outcome would be living like an overload with many big mistakes.

Then there is Heathcliff. I like cats, and the immortal Grace could not have a normal kittycat. I see Heathcliff more like the cat behind the curtains, pulling the strings of the true story. I intentionally did not explain all of her motives. Cats are supposed to be mysterious creatures.

I always found English difficult. In ninth grade, I applied a lot of effort and eventually brought my grades up. I credit part of this to my ninth-grade junior high teacher, Mr. Olpin. I went to college at WPI in Worcester and received a degree in Electrical Engineering (Electrical Engineering is the best kind of engineering). It was a chilly place for a California boy, but I got a fantastic education in life and engineering.

The important part: I was born in San Diego, California, in 1969. I still live in San Diego without plans to move, and I am happily married and have one daughter.

–Bill Conrad, July 2017

I self-published *Interviewing Immortality* five years ago, and many people read it. They all had great things to say, which deeply touched me. In that time, my writing ability improved, and despite an extreme effort to edit away flaws, I uncovered many. So I corrected the writing flaws with this second edition.

The major changes concerned "dialog integration," which is the text and formatting surrounding dialog. I also have the habit of explain a concept and repeating my thoughts by doing it twice. See, I did it again!

I chose not to change the plot because I wanted to preserve the original concept. However, I would have liked to restructure large segments of this book. Grace should have been more organized and less honest. Heathcliff's communications needed to be expanded.

The plot of *Interviewing Immortality* still captivates me, and I am glad I went down the path of making this story public. The sequel *Finding Immortality* is written, and the plot is fantastic. In addition, I have an excellent story for a third book titled *Saving Immortality* and a fantastic concept for a fourth tentatively titled *Living with Immortality*. Please check my website for details.

–Bill Conrad, October 2021

DEDICATION

Why are book dedications always in the front? How does that location help the reader? Do they have the Oscar award thank-you speeches at the beginning of movies? With that in mind, I put my dedication at the end.

I have been fortunate to have had two amazing parents. They were supportive, wonderful, patient beyond words, caring, and loving. Without their support, I would be nothing of consequence. My mother pushed me to keep writing and is my trustworthy beta reader. My father has been an author of many ceramics textbooks and served as an inspiration and role model. My sister is a constant source of encouragement and help. I have been fortunate to have an amazing woman like her in my life.

My wife has been immensely supportive, and without her help and love, this book would not have remained in my mind.

And finally, I dedicate this book to my amazing daughter, Kayla. She makes my life complete.

There is still one person I wish to thank. My pen-pal from New Zealand Emily Rayven has been encouraging and a great friend. I am lucky to have met her and read her amazing stories.

www.ingramcontent.com/pod-product-compliance
Lightning Source LLC
Chambersburg PA
CBHW070454260626
47161CB00004B/1292